I0783939

DOWN TO THE LIAR

A TRUST ME NOVELLA

TRUST ME SERIES
BOOK 2

MARY ELIZABETH SUMMER

MONOCEROS
PUBLISHING

This is a work of fiction. Names, characters, places, and incidents either are the product of the author's imagination or are used fictitiously. Any resemblance to actual persons, living or dead, events, or locales is entirely coincidental.

Text Copyright © 2024-2025 by Mary Elizabeth Summer

All rights reserved. Published in the United States by Monoceros Publishing, LLC, Oregon.

No part of this book may be reproduced in any form or by any electronic or mechanical means, including information storage and retrieval systems, without written permission from the author, except for the use of brief quotations in a book review.

To submit a request, go to maryelizabethsummer.com.

Cover Design: The Killion Group, Inc.

Get new release updates and exclusive content when you sign up for my mailing list at geni.us/theunderground.

1

THE POPULAR GIRL

J*ulep*

I dangle from my fingertips, trying to judge in the darkness how far the soles of my Converse are from the wet pavement. The pavement is always wet in Chicago during the ass-end of March. If it's not snow, it's rain. If it's not snow or rain, it's the bitter tears of California transplants.

"A little help here?" I call out to Dani, who has already leapt effortlessly from the ladderless fire escape to the ground.

"You are perfectly capable of getting down yourself."

Her English has improved over the six short months of our acquaintance. She still has a dubious relationship with contractions, but she's come a long way. I'm not sure that's a good thing, though—gives her too much ammunition to talk back with.

"I am Julep Dupree, grifter, forger, and master of disguise. I am not an acrobat." I shuffle my hands for a better grip. Is it five feet to the ground? Ten? "Besides, I'm allergic."

"To jumping?"

"To breaking both my legs."

"I am unfamiliar with that allergy."

"It's pretty debilitating, actually." I swing my foot toward a nearby Dumpster and catch the edge of it with my toe. If only it were a few inches closer. Or the ground were a few feet closer. "You can look it up when we get back."

Her arms wrap around my legs, warm and sure, and she plucks me off the fire escape as if I were a cat in a tree.

"Thanks." I step out of her hold and wipe my slimy hands on my jeans.

She shrugs an I'm-already-thinking-about-something-else shoulder. I know that's what it means, because she does it a lot. Dani doesn't talk much, so reading her subtler cues is key if you spend significant amounts of time with her. Sadly for me, she's learning English a lot faster than I'm learning Dani.

"I can admit when I'm wrong," I say.

She smirks at me as we walk through the alley toward her skulking, black-with-white-racing-stripes Chevelle. The *since when?* she isn't saying is implied in her smile.

"Okay, I'm never wrong."

"You were wrong about your target. She is not having an affair with that rabbi."

"I was right that she was lying about where she was going. That's mostly right. Mostly right overrules partly wrong. If you're rounding."

"I do not know what *rounding* is, but I am sure you cannot do it to truth."

"You can if your relationship with truth is as sketchy as mine is."

The harsh brightness of security lights guarding the backdoors of buildings spills at regular intervals into the alley. Some are on motion sensors, some flicker as if they're about to die, but all of them bathe us in bleakness as we pass. Dani looks at home in it. Her short-cropped, bone-blonde hair and oil-black leather jacket make as chilling a combination as the security lights beating back against the night. But instead of unnerved, I feel safe, both in the alley and with Dani. She may be a nineteen-year-old mob enforcer, but she shares the same weakness for protecting the innocent that I do. And filthy, rat-infested alleys? They're my preschool playground.

I'm not sure why Dani sticks around. She promised my dad that she would protect me from her boss, but both my dad and her boss are now in prison, so I'd count that as being officially off the hook. She's still here, though— checks on me at the office when I'm there late, assists me in the less savory spying-type jobs, like tonight, and even acts as chauffeur once in a while. I don't pay her, because the first and last time I tried to, she nearly took my head off. Well, she frowned at me and crossed her arms, which for Dani is like throwing a raging hissy fit. So there's nothing in it for her as far as I can see, and that tends to make me nervous.

But to be honest, I'm too grateful for her company to protest. Murphy Donovan, my official partner-in-crime, isn't the best at fieldwork. He gets computers, helps with research and tech stuff. But he's not my other half the way my previous partner Sam was.

Sam's the best hacker I've ever met and he's great at the in-person scams. He's also my best friend—or rather, was my best friend, before he abandoned me for military school.

Dani's the closest thing to backup I have now. And I'll be honest, when she's around, I miss Sam a little less.

Nothing makes me miss Tyler any less.

"What are you going to tell your client about his fiancée's 'affair'?"

I slide into the passenger seat of the Chevelle. "I can't tell him she's secretly taking classes from his rabbi so she can convert to Judaism for him. First, it would ruin the surprise. Second, I might hurl."

Speaking of, I text myself a reminder to send an invoice to my client for his super-secret spying mission. I'll be charging extra for the fire-escape episode. If you're going to pay an investigator to snoop on your fiancée for you, you deserve to get gouged.

"I'll probably tell him she's in a book club or something. He doesn't look like the type who—"

The phone rings while I'm holding it, and a purple orchid user pic appears on the screen.

"That's weird."

"What?" Dani's voice is low and even like always, but there's tension in it that didn't exist a moment ago. She's almost as paranoid as Mike Ramirez, my FBI handler and, technically, foster parent. I've given up assuring them both that the mob boss I took down last October is safely behind bars and not likely to leap out of every shadow. They're both hardwired to believe that anything out of the ordinary is a trap.

"Bryn's calling. She never calls me." I tap the answer button. "Hey, Bryn—I don't have your boyfriend with me, but I'm sure if you switch on his Home Again tracking chip, you'll find him in—"

"Can the snark, Julep," she says. "If I wanted Murphy, I'd call him. I need you."

My eyebrows shoot up. "Really? What for?"

"I have a job for you."

FIFTEEN MINUTES LATER, Dani and I roll up to Cafe Ballou, my coffee haunt and after-school office. The Ballou is its usual self: rickety tables, stuffed chairs, and lacquered bar. The lighting is as moody as the teens still packed around tables, studying feverishly for St. Agatha's infamous midterms. I should be studying for said midterms myself, but my Yale dreams have all been smashed anyway, thanks to last year's Ukrainian mob fiasco. It's all about the benjamins now. Well, and coffee.

I skip the line and put in my usual order with Yaji, my trusty barista. He rolls his eyes at me but starts my drink anyway. He's gotten used to me over the last few months, insofar as someone can get used to me. I like him well enough, even if he only gives me free drinks on my birthday.

Dani follows me as I walk over to the table Bryn and her BFF Skyla have already staked out for us. I sink into the chair across from them, while Dani leans against the wall next to me. I don't have to look to know her eyes are on the room instead of us. But she'll hear every word we say, and that's what's important. The client is my job. Territory is hers.

Speaking of clients, Barbie-doll Bryn looks pissed, which is actually not all that unusual for her, at least when I'm around. Tall, tanned, and gorgeous Skyla, however, looks miserable. And that is not normal. I don't know Skyla very well, but I know enough to describe her as generally sweet and cheerful, if a little on the shy side. She's one of those rare popular girls who gets along with everyone.

Both Bryn's blue and Skyla's brown eyes swing to Dani as we settle in. Bryn knows Dani in passing, but Skyla's never met her before. There's no need to introduce her, though. Dani's notorious at St. Agatha's for her role in the aforementioned Ukrainian mob fiasco. And even if she weren't, she's magnetic and kind of frightening. People tend to forget I'm present when Dani's around. Which is exactly the way I like it most of the time.

"Show me," I say, taking the seat across from Skyla.

Skyla leans back, dropping her watery gaze to her lap. Bryn opens her Bedazzled laptop and turns it so I can see a fairly ordinary-looking Facebook page. But I grow cold as I scroll through the litany of insults, fat jokes, and requests for Skyla to off herself. I'd bet an A in psych class that it's unprovoked, since the content of the attacks all center on Skyla's looks, her likely fabricated sexual exploits, and her worth as a person, rather than referring to specific events. To me, that says someone's hacked off about Skyla's mere existence, not anything she did.

Worse than the attacks themselves, they appear to be coming from multiple Facebook accounts, which indicates a group of bullies. I check the names at the top of each Facebook profile, but none of them ring a bell. They're normal names, like Jo Black, Allie Trask, Kimmy Plith. But I'm fairly familiar with who's who at St. Aggie's, and I don't recognize any of them. The odds on that are not great, so I'm guessing the names are fake to keep the perpetrators from getting caught.

From what I've seen so far, I'm putting my money on a group of rotten and bored teen boys, who have targeted

Skyla as easy prey. That, or she rejected one of them, and he's still butt-hurt about it. In any case, they're not posting about anyone else—only Skyla. And they aren't holding back. The suggestions that Skyla commit suicide in new and interesting ways are nauseating. Which is saying something, because it takes a lot to unsettle me.

"When did it start?" I ask, as Yaji drops off my triple soy caramel macchiato.

"A few weeks ago." Skyla alternates between wringing her hands and tucking strands of her glossy brown hair behind her ear. "I ignored it at first. But it's getting so bad. And now the pictures."

"Pictures?" I say before taking a sip.

Bryn positions the computer so she can click to the right place. When she finds it, I wince. Someone obviously doctored the photo, stretching Skyla's features and body into grotesque configurations.

"It gets worse," Bryn says. She drapes an arm around Skyla. "They reference Skyla's class schedule, describe her hairstyle or what she's wearing on any given day—"

"Which means the cyber-snipers have her in their literal sights," I finish.

Bryn says, "I've been trying to get her to go to the dean for weeks. When they started mentioning her boyfriend, Garrett, in their attack posts, I finally convinced her to come to you."

I tap the table, thinking. "Does Murphy know about this yet?"

Bryn shakes her head, so I text him to get his bespectacled self down here. It's just shy of seven, so I'm pretty sure he's still upstairs in our office above the Ballou. My phone buzzes a second later with a snarky emoji, which I take to mean that he's on his way.

"Have you pissed anyone off lately?" I ask Skyla.

"No." Skyla leans against Bryn. I expected her to elaborate, maybe even get defensive, but she leaves it at a simple negative.

"Any idea at all who it could be?"

She closes her eyes and shakes her head.

Bryn looks at me accusingly. "Isn't it your job to find out?"

"I don't know. Is it?" I study Skyla as I ask. "What exactly are you hiring me to do?"'

"Just make it stop," Skyla says without opening her eyes.

Dani shrugs when I look for her opinion. It's her up-to-you shrug. She has a lot of shrugs.

"What's happening?" Murphy asks when he joins us. He scoots in next to Bryn on the loveseat she's sharing with Skyla. They're an odd couple, especially when seen so close together—like Barbie and Michael Cera instead of Ken.

Bryn angles the computer so Murphy can see the adulterated picture of Skyla. He sucks a breath through his teeth as he clicks through the multiple hater accounts.

"Dang," he says softly, shooting Skyla a sympathetic

look as he leans back in his chair. "That sucks, Sky. I'm sorry."

"Do you think you can find out who's behind this?" I ask him.

"Not sure. Anyone can set up a free email account and start an anonymous Facebook page. We can't tell who's accessing a specific Facebook account unless we have eyes inside their computer."

"I don't care who it is," Skyla says.

"You don't care who it is?" I say, amazed. If it were me, the first thing I'd want to know was who was responsible. "Well, even if you don't, it's the only way to permanently stop whoever's doing it. We could probably get Facebook to shut down their fake accounts, but more accounts would just pop up. You have to pull this kind of thing up by the root. Hacking at its heads is only going to make it worse."

"Whatever. I don't care how you stop it. I just don't want to know."

I guess I can appreciate that. If I could unknow what happened to Tyler, if I could unsee his blood all over my hands, I'd barter my soul away in a second. Knowing is not for everyone.

"We may have to publicly shame them to get them to stop," I point out.

"No." Skyla's eyes pop open and she leans toward me, her face hard. "I don't want that. I'm hiring you to make it stop, but not that way." She shudders, pulling herself together. "Sorry. I don't mean to be so intense about this, but I can't make it any clearer. I don't want to know who it is. I don't want to have to deal with it if I see them in the halls. I still have two years to go in this shallow-ass school. No offense, Bryn."

No offense, Bryn? Murphy and I are shallow-ass St. Aggie's students, too, and we're sitting right here.

"None taken, sweetie." Bryn side-hugs her.

"I just want to get through this," Skyla continues. "I don't want to know anything. I just want you to take care of it."

I chafe at Skyla's restrictions. Making concessions is not how I roll. Truthfully, I'd probably pass on the job if it weren't for Bryn's personal stake in it. She's part of the Julep circle of protection whether or not I like to admit there is such a thing. I owe it to her to at least try to solve her friend's problem. I don't owe it to her enough to do so for free, though.

"A thousand for the retainer, plus expenses," I say. "We charge a hundred an hour for J.D. Investigations services. That's for all of us, not each of us. If we earn out the retainer, I'll bill you hourly from there. If we don't, I'll refund you the remainder."

"Done," Skyla says. "I'll pay whatever it takes. Just fix it."

"That is, in fact, exactly what we do."

WHEN DANI DROPS me off that night at the Ramirezes' house, I ask Mike for information on the aboveboard methods for shutting down cyberattacks. I try not to rely too much on FBI-sanctioned solutions, but sometimes it really is the easiest way to achieve a goal.

"Let me get this straight," Mike says after demolishing a piece of cornbread. "You're asking me for advice? Angela, would you check her temperature? She must have been bitten by a zombie or something."

"Ha. I'm so amused by you right now," I say and scarf another spoonful of Angela's famous mole poblano.

Mike and his wife, Angela, both work odd hours—him as a sometimes-undercover FBI agent and her as a nurse—so dinnertime shifts from four in the afternoon to eight-thirty at night depending on the day.

"Knock it off, Ramirez," Angela says to Mike as she gets up to take her plate to the kitchen. But when she passes me, she rests the back of her free hand against my forehead. "Perfectly normal."

"I'm surrounded by comedians," I say.

"Better than being surrounded by teen-eating sharks," Mike says.

"I'm not sure I'm not surrounded by teen-eating sharks, actually."

"Explain," he says, eyeing me sharply.

So I tell them about Skyla. When I'm done, Angela's expression is a typical mom-like mixture of horrified and sympathetic. "That's awful. That poor girl."

"The first thing I'd do is report it to Facebook," Mike says, slathering butter on a second piece of cornbread.

I lean forward to snag another piece myself. "Whoever's doing this would just create new accounts. We need to shut it down permanently."

"Then you have to find out who's doing it," he says.

"Any ideas on how to do that?" I ask.

"Start with the victim."

"I did. She says she has no idea who's behind it."

"Doesn't mean following her around won't give you leads," he says. "It worked with you."

I chew on that while he chews on cornbread. He has a point. Following me did lead him to Petrov. But then Petrov wasn't trying to hide behind a computer screen.

That night, as I lay in bed, staring up at the ceiling in Mike and Angela's guest room, I flipped through memories of the time before I became Julep Dupree, rescuer of human-trafficking victims. Tyler . . . I will always regret that I happened to him. But at the moment, I feel the loss of Sam more.

We were in fourth grade when we started running the three-card monte scam on our classmates. We were eleven when we played our first false Good Samaritan scam to get out of gym class. We were thirteen when my dad disappeared the first time with no explanation, and all that stood between me and panic was a scrawny, half-black kid in a Clone Wars T-shirt. We were sixteen when he confessed that he was in love with me and put his life on the line to help me save my dad.

I should be brainstorming this job with him, not Mike. He's the best hacker I know, wicked smart and sensitive, all of which I desperately need on this job. But now he's almost a thousand miles away, being brainwashed by military school. If he ever comes back, he won't be my Sam anymore.

My phone rings and I answer.

"Hey, Bryn. What's—"

"Have you checked Facebook tonight?"

"No," I say, sitting up. "Why?"

"Looks like they're going after you now, too."

2

THE PROOF

S*am*

"Seward."

"Sir," I say to the gym mat—standard issue, complete with the Giles Military Academy logo—cushioning me from the heavily varnished gym floor.

"You call that a fly pushup, cadet?"

Lieutenant Walsh doesn't put his boot on my neck, but I'm sure he'd like to. Rumor says he shoved a freshman last year and was suspended for a month. I've only been here for five months, and I can tell already that Walsh gets off on the rumors. It feeds the power he wields over us.

"If you've got enough energy for wool-gathering, Seward, you're not working hard enough. Fifty more."

I swallow a groan. I'll pass out before I give him the satisfaction of hearing me daunted.

But I signed up for this, didn't I? I left Julep alone and

broken after everything that happened to her to come here and learn to be better—stronger, more independent. And damned if I'm going to fail her again. So I move my trembling arms wider and force myself through an additional fifty pushups.

Then I stagger to my feet and straighten to attention. "Would you like another set, sir?"

Walsh grunts at me and moves on to harass another cadet in my unit. I ignore them and start on the jumping jacks portion of my particular hell—*calisthenics*. I like playing sports. I loathe working out.

When the bell rings, Walsh barks us to attention before dismissing us. I grab my gym bag and head for the door.

"Seward."

My shoulders tighten, but I wait while the other students leave the room. When the last cadet has turned the corner, Walsh leans into my space. He's as tall as me, so his nose is mere inches from mine. But instead of screaming at me like you'd expect, he lowers his voice, pitching it as conversational but lacing it with menace.

"You have a real attitude problem, cadet. Comes from your unusually entitled upbringing no doubt." He emphasizes the *unusually* just enough to make sure I hear the implied racism.

I lock my jaw, hold myself back. This isn't the first time he's tried this intimidation routine, and I doubt it will be the last. He has a dyed-in-the-confederate-wool, white-supremacist vibe that reeks of barely restrained violence.

"You smart-mouth me in class again, and you can bet your daddy's last dollar that you'll be out on your ass. Is that understood?"

"Sir, yes sir," I say and salute.

"Dismissed."

I want to slam the lockers lining the military grey walls as I pass them. I'm getting nowhere and putting up with racist assholes for the privilege. I've been here nearly six months, and I haven't learned anything. Not that I have any idea what I expected to learn. Who I am without Julep? That's simple. I'm me without Julep. Did I really need to move halfway across the country to freaking-nowhere Georgia to figure that out?

I bust through the door to my room. James Pollack, my roommate and the only friend I've bothered making, is lying on his bed, tossing a worn football over his head and catching it again.

"What's your damage?" he asks.

"Walsh."

"What'd he do this time?"

"Gave me fifty extra pushups."

Pollack whistles. "Ouch."

"Yeah, ouch."

He tosses the ball again. "You know he rides you because he can't find anything wrong with you. You're too perfect, Seward. You gotta give him something to pick at."

Pollack hasn't heard Walsh's racist bullshit. Walsh is too good at hiding it. I haven't clued Pollack in on what a bigot Walsh is, because Pollack wouldn't understand how something as seemingly innocuous as *unusually* has a racist undertone. It's rare for a white person to get it. Believe me, I've tried explaining it to friends before.

"I'm not giving that jerk anything." I toss my gym bag onto my empty desk.

Come on, Sam. You can do better than that.

I smile at the sound of Julep's voice in my head. I miss her enough that lately I've been holding imaginary conversations with her. I can't decide if that's creepy or just a sign that I'm losing my grasp of the Material Plane. It's probably both.

"Besides a lawsuit," I add.

She winces. *We'll work on it.*

My smile fades. *Enough* is an understatement. I miss her so much it hurts.

"Whatever. I'm starving."

Pollack is always starving.

"Mess hall should still be open."

"You coming?"

We take the back way to the cafeteria to avoid running into Walsh. Pollack picks the route. He's a decent guy, for a white dude from the Deep South—which just goes to show that stereotypes is a game we all play.

We get food and take seats at our unit's table. There are a group of freshmen, or "rats" as the upperclassmen call them, eating silently at the table closest to the trash-cans, despite rows of empty tables with better real estate. They're not allowed to talk during meals, but they always seem pretty cheerful about it. It's like they live for the hazing.

Actually, all of the students of Giles Military Academy seem happy. Relieved even. As if divesting them of indi-viduality alleviates the burden of them having to be *on* all the time, jockeying for social status and pretending they have all the answers. I'm probably the only idiot who got into military school to escape conformity.

"Pollack." A too pretty, black-haired girl with huge blue eyes joins us. She isn't carrying food, so she's not planning on sticking around for long.

"Olson." Pollack raises a fork in greeting.

Olson looks uncertainly at me. "You're Seward, right? The new guy?"

"Newish. I started in October."

"From Chicago?"

Something's up. My inner Julep is on high alert.

"Yes." I can tell by her light southern drawl that she's not a sister from Chi-town. "I have a cousin who says he's heard of you."

I give Olson a thorough once-over. She seems nervous but not aggressive. I don't think she's looking to cause trouble, at least not for me. If anything, she's acting like a potential— Oh.

"I can't help you."

Olson stares at me. "I haven't even told you—"

"It doesn't matter. I'm not the person you're looking for. That person is still in Chicago."

Pollack's gaze cuts from me to Olson and back again. I haven't told him anything about Julep or what happened to get me sent here. As far as he knows, I wanted to come. And it's true enough. My dad may have ordered me into military school, but I didn't argue with him. I needed to distance myself from the past so I could find my way to a better future. Talking about my past didn't seem to be the most effective way to do that, so I never filled Pollack in on the details.

She presses her palms flat on the table. "Look, I don't have anywhere else to turn. You're the only chance I have to get it back."

I tip my chair rearward, thinking. Am I really going to let this girl lay her problems on me? I'm curious, I admit. But I've never had curiosity lead me to anything but trouble.

Ah, hell. "Get what back?"

"My proof."

"Proof of what?"

Olson blinks in confusion before catching on. "No, not evidence. A mathematical proof. Have you heard of Mochizuki, the Japanese mathematician who solved the ABC conjecture?"

"The geometrician?"

"That's the one." Olson's face lights up like I've just given her a cookie. "I can't believe you've heard of him."

"I haven't really. I just saw him mentioned in an article in *Popular Science*. What does this have to do with getting your proof back?"

"I've been wading through Mochizuki's paper on the ABC conjecture. Mathematicians are still testing out his theories to confirm his solution. I was working on just a tiny piece of it, just for practice, you know? But I think I figured something out. Then I showed it to Professor Roth, and he took my composition book, saying he wanted to show it to some colleague for verification. Two days later, I saw he'd announced his "discovery" to the media. He stole my proof."

I can't believe I asked. "How do I know you came up with it first?"

"I can show you my other composition books. I have previous drafts of the proof, all dated. The wording matches his quotes in the article word-for-word. Besides, I'm not the first student he's done this to."

Olson hands me a printout of a news article from three years ago with the headline Student Accuses Academy Faculty Member of Stealing Math Discovery.

"Look, the kid even tried to fight it, but he was crushed in court. The faculty all backed Roth. I can't go to them with this. They'll crucify me."

I scan the article, but it doesn't really change anything.

Truth or not, I'm not in the game anymore. I try to hand it back, but Olson waves it off.

"Keep it," she says. "I have it saved on my hard drive."

"What is going on?" Pollack asks me. "Why is she telling you all this?"

I rub my face. "Because I used to help someone help people. But I wasn't the brains behind that operation. The most I can do is hack into Roth's computer and give it a virus."

"Please?" For a military cadet, she has the big-melty-eyed, damsel-in-distress expression down to a science. "I've done everything else in my power to get it back myself. I even told my unit commander."

"He didn't believe you?" I ask.

"No, he *did* believe me. He said that it was Roth's right to take my proof. That students are like apprentices or some crap."

I feel rage stirring my blood again. "He actually said it was Roth's right?"

"Yes. I don't know what else to do, Seward. If you don't help me get it back, I'm going to have to set fire to Roth's office."

"Don't do that." I lean forward fast enough that my chair legs plunk loudly on the linoleum flooring. "You're the first person they'll suspect."

"I don't care at this point. I can't just let him get away with it."

I really don't need this right now. Every delay is that many more days before I can go home.

You can do it, Sam, Julep whispers.

Even if I could, I don't want to do it without you.

Maybe that's why you should. She smiles in my mind's eye, and I cave.

I take another hard look at the article Olson gave me. There's a picture of the kid sitting in the courtroom. He looks pensive, far too serious for a high-school student. Far too much like me.

"All right, Olson. I'll help you get it back. But I'm warning you up front, I don't really know what I'm doing."

Olson smiles, her expression tight. "You're the best chance I've got. I'll risk it."

"Excellent," Pollack says, clapping his hands together. "What's happening?"

LATER THAT NIGHT, I'm scrolling through Internet search results, none of which address what to do if a teacher steals a student's work. So much for an easy answer. My other option is to call Julep for advice, but I won't do that unless I have to. If I lean on her, it's like I never left. I'll be back to square one.

Of course, that doesn't mean I can't consult the Julep in my head.

It's about time, idiot.

Well? What would you do if you were me?

I'd get a haircut.

Seriously?

Okay, okay. You just gotta break it down into goals. What does your mark want?

Fame, I guess.

Then give it to him.

And like a light turning on, I start to see patterns, a path forward like algorithms and data structures in a computer program. It's just the beginning of an idea. And no matter what direction it goes in, it's not going to be easy. But the idea is solid, and that's more than I had a minute ago.

Why can't you fix me like you fix everything else?

I'm not sure if she's asking me or I'm asking her, but she answers anyway.

Because there's nothing to fix.

I suck in a breath and hold it just to feel something in my chest besides emptiness. I don't often let myself think of our kiss at the formal—the kiss she didn't seem to see coming. But I do now. I close my eyes and feel her in my arms.

"Dude, turn out the light already."

I slouch in my chair, letting go of the breath and the image. Then I shut my laptop lid, putting it to sleep.

3

THE SETUP

*J**ulep*

"Good morning, brindle-coated, dogface bitch," Murphy says as I join him in St. Aggie's computer lab the next morning.

"Skyla's frenemies are notably creative in their insults," I say, snorting in amusement as I hop up to sit on the table across from him.

Brindle-coated. I can't even take that seriously. The other two posts Skyla's antagonizers wrote about me were equally asinine. But the creepy part I can't laugh off is that the posters knew Skyla had met with me so soon after the fact.

Hence our campout in St. Aggie's computer lab. We're starting the job with a Trojan horse scam to see if we can breach the Internet trolls' defenses through their personal computers. That's right—good old-fashioned spyware, baby. God bless governments and creepy corporations.

Ms. Shirley, the computer science teacher and chief overlord of the lab, thinks we're conducting a research experiment on Internet surfing patterns. She has no idea we're actually planting spyware into the computers, phones, and tablets of a couple dozen of Skyla's closest friends, so we can monitor every click and swipe they make over the next few days. No doubt we're violating several school rules, a dozen or so ethical principles, and maybe even a law or two. But hey, if it finds us the culprits, well . . . what's a little loss of privacy among friends?

"If Sam were here, he could hack into the Facebook servers directly and get the IP addresses without breaking a sweat," Murphy says, clacking away on his laptop. But Sam isn't here, is what he doesn't say. He probably knows I'd sense the judgment. Murphy thinks I shouldn't have let Sam leave. Or maybe it's me who thinks that.

"Why bother taking the easy road when the hard way is so much more fun?" I say with a shrug.

"Incoming," Murphy says, nodding toward Bryn, who's hurtling toward me at a velocity that can only mean she's pissed about something.

"Bracing for Bryn-pact in three, two . . . "

He looks annoyed. "Hilarious."

"What the hell, Julep? You put me on the suspect list?" Bryn says when she stalks up to us.

A few months ago, I'd have been irked by the accusation—not because it implies I don't know what I'm doing, which it does, but because I used to hate having to explain every little thing to newbies. But now I'm getting accustomed to playing disreputable-Yoda, which is proof that you can, in fact, teach an old con new tricks.

"First of all, it's not a list of suspects, it's a list of people participating in our *research project*," I say, signaling her to keep her voice down. If she doesn't zip it, she'll tip off Ms. Shirley. "And second, of course I did. I don't want anyone getting suspicious that you're *not* on the list."

Bryn scoffs. "That doesn't make any sense. The others don't know they're on a list."

"Whoever's behind the attacks knows they're doing something wrong, which makes them naturally suspicious of anything unusual happening around them. Especially if it involves computers. They're more likely to trust the legitimacy of this *research project* if they see that Skyla's BFF is participating, too."

"How'd you get everyone to agree anyway?" She folds her arms, her body practically buzzing in irritation.

"The carrot and the stick, like always. The carrot being a ten-dollar gift card to the Ballou. The stick: threatening to cut off their access to the school WiFi."

Murphy looks up. "We did not threaten to cut off their WiFi."

"I may have threatened to cut off Jenna's WiFi," I say.

Murphy's expression is now as aggravated as Bryn's.

"What?" I hop off the table. "She doesn't drink coffee."

Bryn shakes her head. "This better work. Or we'll have betrayed all our friends for nothing."

"Chill out, Judas. In a day or two, we'll have found our bullies, we'll eighty-six the spyware, and no one will be the wiser."

Bryn grabs my arm. "Wait—'found our bullies'? Skyla made it clear she doesn't want to know who's behind it."

Murphy disappears behind his laptop screen again, letting us girls duke it out.

"I'm not planning on telling Skyla who they are," I say, proud of myself for not yanking my arm out of her grasp despite my own growing irritation. See? I can be patient. "But it doesn't change the fact that I need to know. I can't stop them if I don't know what they want." Or more accurately, what they fear.

Bryn clearly doesn't approve of my answer, but it's really not my job to do everything the Bryn Way. If it were, I'd quit that crap job in a hot second.

"Look, I'm hoping it's a superficial clique misunderstanding I can correct with a little leverage. No public humiliation."

"What if it's more than that?"

"I'll worry about that if we get there. I can't come up with a solution before I understand the problem."

"It's time," Murphy says. "You'd better take off, Julep, unless you want to blow the whole thing."

A regrettable outcome of my shenanigans at the end of last term is that everyone is now automatically skeptical if

I'm involved in something. Even though I'm supposedly spearheading this "project," I can't risk one of our marks getting suspicious. I can barely say hi to people in the hallway without them giving me the what's-your-angle eyebrow. So I end up farming out most of my St. Aggie's work to people who owe me favors. It's annoying having to deal with that extra layer between me and the job, and there's been more than one botched assignment I've had to smooth over. I hate taking the risk, especially with Dean Porter continually breathing down my neck. But I'm often too busy with non-school-related cases to do everything myself anyway.

Bryn wordlessly swings her backpack to the floor, fishes out her laptop, and hands it to Murphy.

"Phone and tablet, too." He smiles at her apologetically. She glares at him but produces the phone.

I head out the door, clutching my own laptop on the off chance someone sees me leave the room. Always play the role to its fullest, or one day you'll slip up just enough to get caught. My dad taught me that. Too bad he didn't follow his own advice. He slipped up enough to get caught by the mob, and now he's in the pen with a bum shoulder and a five-year sentence. It could have been worse, though. He could have been dead. Like Tyler.

Thinking about my dad inevitably leads to me thinking about my mom. I still haven't found her. I have no freaking idea where to even start looking, and neither does my dad. I've combed through my student file, but none of the people listed in it are easily traceable. Not even the FBI has records of them, which leads me to really wonder about whoever put together that file. How did they manage to glean even the small crumbs of information they had? And more importantly, *why?* Was it the dean herself? Or was it someone else? And why keep the information in my student file? Did whoever it was *want* me to find it?

Which brings me to Ralph, my dad's bookie and best friend, who is still missing, too. He should have made some kind of contact by now. It's been months. Petrov won't admit to killing him, but that doesn't mean he didn't. Part of me hopes Ralph comes back. A bigger part of me hopes he's cashed out and is lying on a beach somewhere sipping mai tais and binging Korean cookies.

And thinking of Ralph always brings me back to thoughts of Tyler. The boy who drove me to Ralph's when I found out about the mob's involvement in my dad's disappearance. The boy I almost maybe could have loved. The boy who betrayed me. The boy who died instead of me.

My brain shies away from dwelling too long on him. Especially lately. Something will trigger a memory, and I'll flinch. Then anger swirls up, swallowing the memory and the pain. The practical effect is that I've gotten a lot darker lately, and I snap quicker and more often. I know I'm doing it, but I can't make myself stop. Everything irks me these days.

I stop at my locker and shake myself loose from the grip of things I can do nothing about. I'm much better off focusing on the job at hand. And just as I think that, the majority of St. Aggie's girls' tennis team passes me on their way to the computer lab. Skyla's on the tennis team as well, but she tends to socialize with Bryn's group instead. It's not much of a motive for publicly urging someone to off herself, but popularity is a strange animal, and high school can be a pit of vipers sometimes.

I slam my locker door closed and jump when I see the person standing behind it, waiting for me to notice him.

"Good grief, Carter," I say, holding a hand to my chest. "Make some noise next time, will you?"

"Sorry." He doesn't look sorry. He looks like a weasel with a five-o'clock shadow and a greasy tangle of dark hair. "Murphy sent me to get your computer. He wants to add the receiver to your hard drive, so you can help him sort through the data."

I hand him the computer. "You were friends with Sam, right?"

He nods, though on him it's more a head-duck than a nod.

"Do you still talk to him?"

"Not really," Carter says. "He's not on the forums much anymore. Kind of a shame. He always seemed to know the answer."

My chest tightens, so I nod back instead of speaking.

He starts off down the hall, but I stop him. "Thanks, Carter. For helping with the job. You didn't have to."

He keeps his eyes downcast as he says, "I know her." Then he scurries away before I can say anything else too far outside his comfort zone.

"Ms. Dupree. Loitering in the hallway, I see."

Speak of the devil. Dean Porter, St. Agatha's titian-haired dean of students, and my personal nemesis. I want to roll my eyes at her, but the last thing I need is for her to haul me into her office. If I never see the inside of that floral monstrosity again, it will be too soon.

"I believe fourth period is still currently in session."

I hand her the pass I always keep on my person. I have a stack of them in my bag for just such an emergency. I am an expert forger, after all.

The dean doesn't bother examining the pass. She knows it's as fake as the IDs I unloaded on her desk last October. But she also knows she can't prove it without talking to the teacher whose signature I forged, and Mr. Ludzinski owes me a favor. Even if she could get him to back her up, I'm a protected species at St. Aggie's these days. President Rasmussen likes me, which means I can get away with pretty much anything short of setting the library on fire.

"Get to class." She levels her bulldog gaze at me. But as soon as her back is turned, I smile. She's carrying her laptop, and she's headed toward Ms. Shirley's computer lab. It was too good an opportunity to pass up. A window into the dean's personal computer? Yes, please. Maybe I'll find out she knows more about my family than what's in that file.

I'm about halfway to fourth period when I pass the door to the chapel. Skyla is kneeling in front of the statue of St. Nicholas and lighting a candle. I almost keep going. She hired me to make the attacks stop, not to counsel her through the experience. But Mike's advice echoes in my brain: follow the victim. Maybe I can get something out of her while she's in the mood for confession.

I kneel next to her, clumsily making the sign of the cross. I don't pray very much, or, you know, ever. But I can fake the motions well enough.

"He's the patron saint of thieves," I say, indicating the statue. "We go way back, St. Nick and I."

"He's also the saint of children," she says quietly, not looking at me.

"You say 'tomato' ... "

"What can I do for you, Julep? I've already served you the privacy of all of my friends on a silver platter."

"If they're not responsible for the attacks, they have nothing to fear from me. I'll push the deactivate button on the spyware myself the second this is over."

"Well then, what do you want? It's kind of hard to hold a conversation with you and God at the same time."

"I get that a lot." I light my own candle, wondering where the patron saint of children was when Tyler was shot. "Are you sure you don't want me to make it public?

Taking down your attackers, I mean. I can ruin them for you."

She sighs. "And what good would that do?"

"They would never do it to you, or anyone else, ever again. You'd be doing the school a public service."

She doesn't respond for several minutes, but then she settles back on her heels and faces me.

"I'm not interested in doing anyone any favors. I just want to survive this. I'm not strong like you or Bryn."

"Then you can lean on us. You're not alone in this, if you don't want to be."

Skyla's gaze drops to her hands lying folded and limp in her lap. "I know." She seems to be thinking something she's not sure how to say. I wait for her to figure it out. I have time.

"Garrett's been very supportive. Not just during all this awfulness, but since we started dating last year. My parents . . . they've always been so wrapped up in their music careers and each other, I've only ever been an afterthought to them. I've spent holidays alone since I was six. But then Garrett came along and made me feel taken care of. I don't want to lose that. I just want to go back to what it was like before all this started happening. Can you do that?"

She's asking it with a genuine tone rather than a challenging one. Her expression is pleading for understanding. And I do understand. I can tell you from personal experience that notoriety is not all it's cracked up to be.

"I will try." I reach for her hand and squeeze it. She smiles for the first time.

AT HALF PAST BORING O'CLOCK, I lean back in my desk chair in the Ballou office, rubbing my eyes and fighting a yawn. This paper on the importance of textiles in the English industrial revolution is about to choke the life out of me. The evening started so promising with sending out invoices and logging received checks from past clients. But then I remembered this awful paper is due next week. Just wrap me up in tweed and smother me already.

I decide to take a walk, since I don't have to check back into Casa de Ramirez for another hour. I don't have a particular destination in mind, so it shouldn't surprise me when the 'L' and my feet transport me to my old stomping grounds. I wave at Fred, my former lobby-neighbor, as I pass the apartment building I lived in with my dad and continue on, retracing worn routes to favorite haunts.

Chicago's wet nights smell like a mixture of oil, rain, and newsprint. I get a strange feeling when I smell it. I imagine it's similar to the feeling kids get when they smell their mom's perfume.

I take a left into the alley where I confronted Mike for following me. I stop for coffee at the diner I took him to afterward to hear his story. I pass my dad's favorite Italian restaurant and almost go in to say hi to Mr. Pacini, the proprietor. In the end, I decide against it. He'd have too many questions I don't have good answers for right now.

I close the loop of memory lane back at the front door of the moldering apartment building. Across the street, the Chevelle cools its tires in the exact same spot it sat in six months ago when I'd gotten my first glimpse of Dani. She's there as well, leaning against the car and watching me.

She comes over to me, her expression unreadable.

"It is raining," she says.

"Is it."

She leads me back to the Chevelle, and I follow without argument. When we get in, she doesn't start the ignition.

"Would you like to talk?" she says.

I must be bad off if Dani is offering to listen to me wallow in my angst.

"It looks worse than it is," I say, feeling the familiar anger stirring again.

She fiddles with the steering wheel. She'd probably rather be facing Petrov again than having this conversation.

"I know how it is to lose everything," she says.

"I didn't lose everything," I say, fidgeting with my sweater cuffs. It's a technicality I'm trying to hide behind, but it doesn't fool her any more than it does me. I can tell by her expression when she turns to really look at me.

"You con yourself into believing you are fine, but it is okay if you are not."

I frown at her. "You'd never let yourself admit weakness, but you're encouraging me to?"

"It is not a weakness to ask for help."

The anger wants me to snap at her—to throw the double standard in her face, to tell her to mind her own damn business. But then I think of the tattoos hidden beneath her coat and wonder which ones represent which losses she had no help processing. She had no one. I at least have her. That's what she's saying, and I can't pretend I don't hear it.

The anger recedes. She is the only person who's managed that particular miracle. And as much as I crave the anger, I'm relieved that I can let it go—at least when I'm with her.

"You're right. I'm not fine," I say, swallowing against the boulder in my throat that's making my eyes water. I drop my gaze to my lap. "But that doesn't change the fact that I have a job to do."

She nods. "What can I do?"

But that's the problem, isn't it? Letting people help me comes with a cost. It's why I'm not okay in the first place. Tyler's death is on me. Sam's exile is my fault, as well. Both of them just wanted to help. But before I recover my voice enough to point that out, Murphy calls.

I clear my throat and answer. "Did you find anything?" I ask without preamble.

"No. Nobody we hacked has logged in to those Facebook accounts."

Dang it. I was hoping we could have this wrapped up in a day or two.

"But I did find something interesting," he continues. "I was looking back through the date-time stamps of the hate posts to see if I could pick up a pattern."

"There was a pattern?"

"None of the posts were uploaded at the same time."

"So? They were probably posting from different places randomly."

"That's what I thought at first, but when I looked closer, they weren't uploaded randomly. They were added linearly, one post moments after the previous one, over different accounts. All the accounts. And each series of posts was always uploaded to each of the accounts in the same order."

"Murphy, what are you saying?"

"I'm saying I don't think it's a group. I think it's just one person."

4

THE SETUP

The computer lab at Giles is decent. Unlike Ms. Shirley's lab back at St. Agatha's, the room is spare and lit with fluorescents, with long rows of cheap, laminate-fiberboard tables weighed down by matching monitors from at least five years ago. After-market cable and keyboard trays keep things military-grade tidy, and the carpet-tiled flooring—a checkerboard pattern of variegated stripes in the school's colors—absorbs the sound from the clacking keys while having a tight enough pile to allow the plastic rollers on the chair legs to glide smoothly over it.

The tech is at least as good as St. Agatha's, which means it's nowhere near as good as my equipment at home. It's frustrating trying to do anything here when I could do it in half as much time at home. But at least I still have my laptop with most of the social engineering programs I either bought, pirated, or built, which is better than nothing. I use the school lab for small-scale tasks that I don't want traced back to me.

I've spent the morning creating an Internet presence (website, socials, reviews, history) for a fake research symposium in mathematics. The hardest part was securing a conference center this late in the academic cycle. We lucked out that Atlanta's local trainspotting group didn't garner enough interest this year to host their annual convention.

Getting presenters was a piece of cake, though. With Olson's input on which mathematicians Roth would be most impressed by, I simply emailed them each a personal invitation to present, saying that a spot had suddenly opened up and the first alternate we emailed would get to fill it. I also name-dropped the other mathematicians Olson listed, hinting that they had already confirmed attendance and sent in their papers. Some have yet to RSVP, but most of them will agree. Especially since I implied that the mathematics department at MIT is not only sponsoring the conference, but also looking to recruit a new director from its presenters.

"Seriously, I don't see how this could possibly work." Olson is hovering over my shoulder, watching me add fictional workshops to the mostly make-believe schedule on the conference website. I save the update, and ALT+TAB to Twitter so I can hashtag the hell out of it.

"The more places the conference exists online, the more legitimate it will seem. We're not selling an actual conference, just the illusion of one."

"Have a little faith, Olson," Pollack says. "He's a professional." Then to me, he says, "You are a professional, right?"

"I'm a hacker. But if it helps, sure, I'm a professional."

"Oh, God." Olson hangs her head, her long, dark braid brushing my keyboard.

I twist my chair to address her face to face. She needs the patented Julep-client pep talk. I wish I'd paid more attention when Julep gave it.

"Listen, I've seen so many cons succeed from a straight-up bluff with zero actual substance. That's the point. Conning someone is selling something that doesn't exist—gaining their confidence that you're legit, that you're a friend, an expert they can trust. In reality, you aren't any of those things. You *don't* have the pig you're trying to sell. That violin you claim is worth a million bucks? Just a knock-off you found at Goodwill. In this case, the conference isn't based on anything real, but that doesn't mean people won't believe it. Especially people desperate to gain professional respect and possibly a job at MIT."

"But how do we know Roth's going to buy it?"

"Because I'm good at what I do," I say.

"Even if you manage to pull it off, I don't understand how this is going to get me my proof back."

Pollack sprays himself in the eye with a compressed-air keyboard duster. He jerks away and blinks rapidly.

I snatch the can from him. "We're not trying to get your proof *back* exactly. We're discrediting Roth so that when you're ready to come forward with it, you can."

"This is all just so. . . illogical."

"Human nature is the opposite of logic." I gesture at Pollack.

"Hey," he says, offended. But then he nods. "Yeah, all right."

Olson sighs, pinching the bridge of her nose. "Okay. I said I didn't have any choice, and I still don't. But if this actually works, I'll be buying stock in unicorns."

A shiny-faced rat appears in the doorway. "Cadet Seward. Lieutenant Walsh wants you in his office."

Brilliant.

"I'll be right there," I say.

After the rat salutes me and leaves, Pollack gives me a covert look, assessing my reaction. He plays dumb, but he sees more than he lets on.

I log out of all the relevant websites and clear the browser history. Don't leave an easy trail unless you want the mark to follow it, Julep would say.

"You want me to come with?" Pollack asks.

"And do what?" I finish packing up. "Thanks, though."

Olson senses something's off, but she doesn't say anything—just watches me with keen blue eyes. Pollack pockets the compressed-air keyboard duster.

When I get to Walsh's office, the arrogant bigot is leaning back in his chair with a self-satisfied smirk on his face. Two of his "teaching assistants," who could easily double as neo-nazi thugs, stand at attention at either end of the back wall, staring off into the distance like thermoplastic GI-Joe action figures.

Walsh keeps a cadre of upperclassmen on his personal detail. He uses them to intimidate people. I hate to admit that it's working, but, well. It is.

"It appears you've been busy," Walsh says as he slaps a manila folder on the desk between us.

I open it to see pictures of me talking to Olson in the mess hall, me and Pollack and Olson in the computer lab, even close-ups of the computer screen I'd had up and running while we were setting up the symposium con that someone sitting behind us must have taken. I make a mental note to sit in the back row from now on. Come to think of it, we always sat in the back in Ms. Shirley's class. Julep must have arranged it that way for this reason.

"What are you insinuating?" I say. "Working in the computer lab is against regulations now?"

"No," he says, unperturbed. "But I think the content of that work might raise some serious questions with the board."

"Then report me." It's not like I'm getting what I thought I would out of this damn military school experience anyway. I might as well go home now.

"Ah, but it isn't just you, is it? Who is that with you? James Pollack?"

I stare at him. Is he really threatening my friends now?

"Lucky for you," Walsh continues. "I'm not interested in exposing you just yet. I could use a boy like you."

I almost choke on my outrage. "What makes you think I'd ever do anything for you?"

He grins. "Because a word from me will get you both expelled."

I desperately battle back the overwhelming urge to tell him exactly where he can shove his intimidation tactics.

"Careful, Seward. I have ways of getting what I want that don't involve wasting the administration's valuable time." He doesn't gesture to the goons behind him, but his meaning couldn't be clearer. Do what he wants, or someone's getting a little extracurricular boxing practice. He probably means me, but can I risk him cornering Pollack in a darkened classroom some night when no one's around?

Easy, Sam. I can almost feel Julep's hand on my arm. *Devious beats obstinate every time.*

"What exactly do you want from me?" I ask through clenched teeth.

"I want you to help me with a problem."

"I'm guessing this is a people problem we're talking about."

He frowns. "I'd watch that mouth if I were you." He taps the folder on his desk. "I own you, son. The sooner you get that through your thick, Halfrican skull, the better."

My hands clutch into fists but I have nowhere to swing them.

"I need you to keep an eye on Olson for me."

That's. . . not what I expected.

"Olson? Why?"

"That's my business and none of yours."

"Keep an eye on her how? Keep her out of trouble? Spy on her? What?"

"Just keep an eye on her. For now."

I study his face for several long seconds. It's not something I ever want to do again. Just looking at him makes me feel polluted. The hatred in his eyes is real, and it leaves me with no doubt of his ability to follow through on his threats.

And all he's asking is for me to keep tabs on Olson? That's not hard, since I'm pulling this job for her. She's going to be in my back pocket for the next week at least. It bothers me that I don't know why, but it's not asking for much. If it turns into something else, something unacceptable, then I'll have to adjust. But for now, I just need Walsh off my back.

Devious beats obstinate. . .

"Fine," I say.

"'Sir,'" he says and smirks at me.

"Sir."

I may not be able to punch him, but I can imagine myself punching him right?

ROTH, I discover, is teaching differential equations to a group of juniors when I slip into the back of his classroom. It's not so many students that I go unnoticed, but it's not so few that I disrupt the lecture either.

Roth is a balding man in his late forties who looks enough like Leonard Nimoy to be his son. I don't instinctively dislike him, but my gut isn't as good at judging marks as Julep's is. And anyway, who doesn't like Leonard Nimoy? Not that it matters what I think about Roth. Too much feeling gets in the way. The cautionary tale for that being Tyler—he fell in love with his mark, and he died because of it.

At the end of class, I approach the lectern with confidence. "Mr. Roth?"

"Doctor."

"Sorry?"

"Dr. Roth."

Put him on the defensive—check.

"I'm Sam Seward, your new teaching assistant. I'm a big fan of your research, sir. Your paper on the twin primes conjecture was impressive. I'm a transfer from St. Agatha's in Chicago. I told my parents that I needed to be at Giles if I wanted to get the best education I could in math. And I want to be an anabelian geometrician, sir, so it's important that I study with the best."

Flatter shamelessly—check.

"There must be some mistake. I didn't ask for a new TA."

"Well, I didn't want to be the one to tell you, but your last TA, Olson, turned in her notice. The director didn't tell me why, sir, but I gathered that she was pretty upset when she resigned."

Deliver implicit threat—check.

"Oh. That's a shame. Then I guess I could use the help." He gathers a stack of papers from his lectern and hands it to me. "Here's the last class's quizzes and the answer key. Deduct points if they neglected to show adequate work."

I manage to keep from rolling my eyes despite myself. Forcing students who know what they're doing to show work has always been a pet peeve of mine. But I take the stack regardless and sit down at a nearby desk in the now empty room to grade them.

So far, so good. He's accepted my story at face value. I'm playing the role of roper in a wire game. It's my job to get him to the conference and presenting with no time to prepare. I'll feed him a tale about an MIT professorship on the table for the hottest presenter at the conference. He has to think it's a sure bet, and then when he presents, we'll expose him as the fraud he is to his colleagues. The school will have to fire him, and Olson will have her chance to unveil her proof when she's ready.

Is it a perfect plan? No. For one thing, Julep's usually the roper. But I'll do what I can.

"Mr. Seward?"

"Yes, sir?" I look up from the tests.

The door at the back of the lecture room bursts open and Olson stalks in, face red with fury. "You stole my proof!"

I leap out of my chair and block her from hurling herself at Roth.

"What the hell do you think you're doing?" I hiss at her.

She tries to push past me to get at Roth. "You stole my proof, you shark, and I want it back."

I glance back at Roth, who has frozen in place, pale and unmoving. It's clear he's not going to react, thank the great grifter in the sky, as Julep would say. So I grab Olson by the shoulders and hustle her back up the aisle toward the door.

"This isn't over!" she shouts as I shut the door behind us.

"Seriously, what the hell?" I shake her, hoping to knock some sense into her.

She drops the act, grinning. "How was that?"

I yank her behind a nearby hedge. "Never drop character that close to a mark ever again. And never go off book without consulting me. What the hell were you thinking?"

"I was helping."

"That was not helping! That was unscripted! You could have ruined the whole con."

She gives me a lopsided shrug. "Sorry. But it felt damn good."

I pinch the bridge of my nose to stave off the start of a headache. "Now I get why Julep hated working with rookies. How did you even know I was here?"

"I didn't. That was just luck."

I swear under my breath. "Well, your luck just ran out. Do anything like that again, and I walk."

"Okay, jeez. No need to get bent out of shape about it."

"No need to—? I'm only in this to help you. If you don't care about the outcome, then why should I?"

"I do care," she says, finally sobering. "And I'm grateful for your help, I am. I won't improvise without consulting you again."

I'm still irritated. "There are too many variables in a wire game. The whole thing depends on everyone doing their part to a hundred-percent perfection. It's why Julep never uses them herself if she can help it. It involves too much trust."

"You can trust me," she says quickly. Too quickly. "I didn't know that the plan was so easily derailed. I'll take your direction seriously from now on, I promise."

"My ass is on the line as much, if not more, than yours

is. If this phony conference is traced back to me, I'm screwed." Walsh made that clear as crystal, though Olson doesn't need to know that. "Which is why I'm being so obsessive about sticking with the plan. I don't want any of us getting expelled over this."

She nods, her expression earnest. "I understand. I'm sorry."

I finally relax, letting go of my grip on her arm. I didn't realize I'd been touching her this whole time. Um, awkward. I try not to be obvious about it, but I think she notices anyway.

"Well, I'd better let you get back in there," she says, her blue eyes deep and soft, the leaf-filtered sunshine dappling her face with radiant freckles.

"Yeah," I say.

She pauses before leaving the shade of our hiding spot. "You're pretty cool, Seward."

And before I can respond to that, she jogs off around the side of the building and out of sight.

THE CRUSH

*J*ulep

Valerie Updike. Notorious gossip and cattiest person alive. Also my current conversational companion. She gets up to go to the bathroom, and I rub my temples to stave off the headache blooming behind my eyeballs. Yaji smiles and shakes his head at me.

So far, I haven't managed to get very much out of our good friend the gossip. No one knows who's pranking Skyla or why. Skyla is universally liked and respected. She's not the best player on the tennis team, but not the worst either. She has pretty good grades, but she's not in the top ten percent, which means she's not a threat to any wannabe valedictorians, not that she's a senior anyway, so even if she were in the top ten percent, the valedictorian theory would be a stretch.

She doesn't have any siblings, jealous or otherwise.

She's squeaky clean, but not so squeaky as to be obnoxious. At this point, the only person with an axe to grind against Skyla is *me* for making it so hard to pin down who her enemies are.

"Well, girl, I gotta bounce." Val springs back to our table with a boundless energy incongruous with her tiny frame. She dashes bejeweled fingers through her pixie cut as she scoops up her purse and kisses me on the cheek. "Red 7 waits for no woman."

Pretty sure Red 7 is a salon, but I couldn't swear to it. In any case, that was an hour wasted. I text Murphy, who's upstairs in the office, running background checks on Skyla's closest friends.

"Oh, there is something, actually," Val says just before walking out the door. "One of the tech geeks is in love with her. What's his name? Carlton? Carlisle?"

"Carter?" My hand tightens around my phone.

"That's it," she says. "Carter. Hope that helps."

Valerie takes her leave as a thousand angry hornets zoom around in my head. Carter. Murphy's tech-club buddy. There's no way Murphy didn't know about Carter's crush. Which means either he's a complete idiot, or his loyalty to Carter is greater than his loyalty to me. Murphy's been working with me long enough now to know better, which means it's a loyalty issue. That boy is so dead.

I stomp all the way upstairs to the office and slam the door behind me. Murphy jumps.

He takes one look at my face and sighs. "Someone told you about Carter?"

I can feel steam coming out of my ears. "The point is, *you* should have told me about Carter."

"It isn't relevant. Carter would never—"

"He had his greasy, weasel hands on my laptop, Murphy! My laptop! He could have done anything to it."

"I'm sure he didn't." Uncertainty flickers across his face. "I'm pretty sure he didn't."

"Well, thanks. I feel so much better now." The level of incompetence I put up with is staggering sometimes.

Murphy frowns at me. "Having a crush on a popular girl does not make you a sociopath."

Ah, now I get it. This isn't a loyalty problem. It's actually a Bryn thing. Carter is the Murphy from last October —hopeless nerd pining after the popular girl. Only Murphy paid me and Sam to help him out. Now Murphy's dating the popular girl, and he's happy. But Bryn's still popular and Murphy's still a nerd, so at heart, he still identifies with Carter.

Knowing all this, I should let him off easy. But will I? Hmmm, let me think about that for a mi— No.

"The problem is not that Carter has a crush on Skyla, Murphy. The problem is that you knew and you didn't tell me." My anger seems to be stuck at volcanic. "From now on, if you know something that connects in any way to a job we're working, you tell me. Is that clear?"

"Crystal." He turns his back on me.

My phone rings. I answer without looking at the caller ID.

"What?" I snarl.

"Whoa, Dupree. What's got you in a snit?" Mike says.

"I'm not in a snit. I'm smacking down one of my minions."

"You know I hate it when you call me that," Murphy says.

I ignore him. "What do you want, Mike?"

"I need your help on a case," Mike says.

"Right now?" I mouth the words *text me his address* at Murphy, who shoots a glare at me but still picks up his phone to find Carter's info. "What kind of case?"

"I'll tell you when we get there."

I sigh. "I don't have time to play criminal informant with you at the moment. I'm engaged in some serious damage control on my own job."

"Guessing that has something to do with why you're being unduly harsh to Murphy."

"I'm not being harsh." I glance through the window and see Mike's Honda parked on the street. "Wait, you're here?"

"I told you I need your help. Come on. Should only take an hour or so."

I rub my face. "Fine. I'll be down in a minute."

I hang up and grab my coat and bag.

"He didn't do it, Julep."

"I don't care if he did it or not. I care that you hid it from me."

"Not telling you is not the same as hiding it."

"Can you honestly say that it didn't once occur to you that telling me about Carter's crush on Skyla might change my approach to the job?"

Murphy doesn't answer, which is all the answer I need.

"You have to trust me, Murphy, or this partnership is never going to work."

He doesn't argue, but his frown is as firm as ever. I suspect this is not going to be our last discussion on this issue.

"I have to go," I say. "Try not to flush the entire job down the toilet while I'm gone."

Okay, that might have been a little harsh, but I'm still too mad to take it back. I stomp back down the stairs and out into the street without so much as a wave to Yaji.

"Nice to see you, too," Mike says when I slam into the front seat of his car.

"You're welcome," I snap for his missing thank-you.

He drives us to the Water Tower Place mall. I follow him into the atrium without comment, still fuming over Murphy's complete lack of professionalism. But once we infiltrate the food court, I get tired of flying without instruments.

"What exactly are we doing here, Mike? Is one of these storekeepers secretly laundering money or something?"

"Not exactly." He leads me to the nearest jewelry store.

"Is it a jewel heist? You think it's an inside job? I can probably squeeze the salespeople to—"

Mike shakes his head. "I need you to help me pick out an anniversary present for Angela."

My jaw drops. "I thought you said you needed my help on a case!"

"I do." He looks at the glass cases like they're full of sphinx riddles. "You know how to read people. You've been living with Angela for several months now. I figure if anyone can tell me which of these dangly, sparkly things she likes, you can."

"Oh, for crying out loud, Mike." I take one look at the case and point at a three-strand-twist Tahitian pearl necklace with matching earrings.

He wears a relieved, satisfied smile as he pays the clerk far too much money for the set. I purposefully wait until we're out of the mall before I say, "Of course, if you wanted to get her something she'd really love, you'd have bought her that outdoor pizza oven she's been drooling over for weeks now."

Mike winces. "Ouch. You are ruthless when somebody crosses you."

I have never been accused of an overabundance of ruth, that is true. But I still don't have to dignify this rude observation with a response.

"Come on, it's not just me and Murphy. What's really eating you?"

Tyler's dead. Because of me. And I can't fix it. And none of this—none of it—is fair.

But I can't say any of that. It sticks to my tongue like cement. So instead I say something else equally true. "It's this whole job. It irks me."

"That's not like you. You're the only person I know who never lets a case get personal. Well, except. . ."

He wisely trails off. We don't talk about that night. Ever. I still have some issues with him over how that all went down. Besides, it's too close to the truth of why I'm so angry all the time. I don't need a shrink to tell me that I'm not over what happened to Tyler. And I'm not encouraging Mike to send me to more therapy by admitting as much.

"I know it's not like me, but there it is. It irks me."

"Do you know why?"

"Something about it is just off." Which is truth enough. Something is off about this job, and it's bugging the crap out of me.

"Is it the nature of the crime? Sometimes that can affect even the most hardened agent."

"A: I'm not an agent. B: While I think the slimeball responsible for those posts deserves to be slow-roasted over a bed of burning napalm, it's not the worst thing I've ever seen. I mean, words can kill faster than bullets—nobody knows that better than a grifter. But the crime isn't what's bothering me. It's something else. Something I missed."

"Would it help to go over the facts?"

"I don't know. Not yet."

"Well, I'm here when you're ready."

My inner grifter winces at the deeper meaning. I don't want his fatherlike support. I never asked for it, and I don't deserve it. I want to say that he can take his offer to talk and shove it, but I remember my heart-to-heart with Dani last night, and my anger ebbs to a low simmer.

I know it's not Mike's fault I'm so messed up. And honestly, it's not Murphy's fault either. I should probably apologize. To all of them, really. But instead of saying anything, I stare out the window, watching in silence as we exit onto the freeway.

"WHAT ARE WE LOOKING FOR?" Dani asks. It's a few minutes shy of eight-thirty, and she's just boosted me up over the wall surrounding Carter's house and dropped down next to me on the other side.

"I don't know." I can barely see her outline in the darkness. "Anything related to Skyla or the Facebook accounts, I guess. A tell-all diary wouldn't hurt."

She nods, tersely, which is exactly what I need right now. Silent obedience. I'm still wrestling with my anger issues, and the less anyone talks around me right now, the better.

"I'll distract Carter as long as I can," I continue. "You sneak in and get the goods."

"I do not read as well as you do."

"Maybe not, but you don't have a legitimate reason for ringing the doorbell either."

"Which one is his room?"

"No idea. Good luck."

I peel off from Dani, who dutifully circles the house in search of Carter's room. I walk boldly up to the front door and push the intercom button. I technically should have buzzed from the front gate and been let in properly, but I wanted to get the lay of the land with Dani before forging ahead with the plan.

"Julep?" Carter says from the intercom. "How did you get in here?"

"I jumped the fence. Look, Carter, I've got a bone to pick with you."

I hear a staticky sigh over the speaker. "All right. Give me a second."

Dead bolts, chains, and locks click open one after the other. Seriously, you'd think this guy lived in a penitentiary or something. My dad's and my apartment in the west-side projects didn't have nearly as many locks.

"What's up with the security?" I ask, mostly because I'm stalling. I don't really care why his parents are paranoid.

"Mom's a federal judge. And a single parent."

"I suppose that makes sense. Can I come in?"

He pulls the door back just wide enough to admit me and shuts it directly after. If he tries to lock anything, I'll kick his geeky butt. But he doesn't.

"I know why you're here," he says.

"Murphy called you?" I'm going to kill that nerd.

"No, but I knew it was only a matter of time before you figured it out."

Oh. Well, Murphy can live on another day, I guess.

"Why didn't you come clean about crushing on Skyla at the beginning?"

He ducks his head. "Because it's embarrassing. And I know I'm not the one doing it, so I thought I didn't need to tell you. I realize how ridiculous that sounds, especially since I was sure you'd find out on your own anyway."

"You realize that you're now my number-one draft pick for douchebag, right? Had you told me on your own, you might have been just a possibility. Now you're the probability."

"Well, I'm not the one harassing Skyla. And if you don't believe me, then the person who is harassing her will keep going. I don't want that for her."

My gut says he's telling the truth, but then my gut has been wrong before. Like Mike, for example—my gut was all kinds of wrong about him. Guts are notoriously unreliable, and every good con artist takes his gut feeling with a grain of salt. But a grifter is, by nature, a gut-follower, and after all, there is no such thing as a safe bet.

"Murphy's already scanned every device I own," he continues. "What else can I do to prove it to you?"

I pull out my phone and swipe through a few screens to bring up my case notes. "You can alibi out."

"How?"

"Prove to me that you were nowhere near an electronic device at eight-thirteen last Tuesday night, or seven-thirty-four the Saturday night before that, or—"

As I watch, I get Facebook notifications that the abusive accounts are posting more vitriol against Skyla.

"What the—?"

Carter crosses his arms. "Even if I could prove I was swimming the English Channel Tuesday night, I could have easily scheduled those posts ahead of time."

I give him a sour look. "So much for alibiing out."

"Look, I don't mind being a suspect."

"Mark."

"Whatever, I don't care. I just want you to catch whoever it is and make them wish they were never born. So as long as you don't rule out everyone else, I'm fine with it. Investigate me all you want."

"It is not him," Dani says, coming up from behind Carter.

Carter yelps in surprise and turns too quickly, smacking into the wall.

"H-how did you get into my house?" he splutters.

"Through your bathroom window. You will need a new screen, by the way."

Carter gapes at her. "I've changed my mind. I don't want you investigating me."

"What do you mean, it's not him?" I ask Dani.

She hands me a sketchbook flipped open to about halfway through. Carter makes a grab for it, but Dani blocks him with a warning look. She gets antsy when people move too fast.

The sketchbook shows panel after panel of graphic-style storyboarding. It's actually not bad. It's not Marvel quality, but it's not bad. More to the point, it shows a more dashing version of Carter ninja-slashing through a horde of masked invaders and saving the damsel in distress—the damsel being a pretty faithful rendering of Skyla.

"This isn't proof," I tell her, handing the sketchbook back to a mortified Carter.

She raises an eyebrow at me. The eyebrow says Oh, please—a child could tell he's not involved. Stop wasting everyone's time.

"Fine," I relent in a huff. To Carter, I say, "But you'd better not leave town."

When I realize how cop-like I sound, I make a face. Dani's lips tilt up at the corner, which is her way of busting up laughing. I give her a dirty look, but it doesn't make her stop.

"Let's go."

"Where?" She opens the door for me. We both ignore Carter.

I sigh heavily. "I guess it's down to the wire."

DANI DROPS me off at the Ballou so I can get my stuff. She offered to drive me home after, but I've still got an hour till curfew and I want to do some strategizing before heading back to Mike's house.

I drop into the comfy, thrift-store-fabulous armchair I usually reserve for clients and prop my feet on my desk. The wire. As if this job weren't bad enough already.

The wire game, for those of you following along at home, is about convincing a mark you can guarantee he'll win the lottery as long as he pays *you* for the ticket, rather than buying it like he normally would.

In the telegraph days, when small delays between events and reporting of those events were common, cons would set up fake betting parlors and trick a mark into plunking down all his money on a racehorse they said they knew in advance would win, when in fact, they knew the horse would lose. The mark would bet big money on the "sure thing" only to forfeit all that money to the cons when the "winning" horse actually lost. The cons running the scam would then split the cash and move on to the next town.

The beauty of the scam is that the mark can't go to the cops without admitting he was trying to place an illegal bet. It's a neat little trick that netted a lot of people some easy money. But it's not without its drawbacks.

For one thing, it requires a lot of people to pull it off—people who can turn on you, mess up their parts, or just plain not show up. Marks are easy to lead. Associates are not.

For another, I've never successfully run a wire game before. I attempted it exactly once, and it blew up spectacularly in my face (refer to previous comment re: associates).

I normally wouldn't touch a wire game with a ten-foot cattle prod. But with this much distance between me and the mark, the wire game is pretty much my only option. It lets me lure the mark out of hiding with the promise of a guaranteed sweet reward and then snag them in a net—the Internet, that is. The telegraph may be long gone, but people are the same. For one thing, they're still far too trusting of technology. And I can tell you from experience that a mark will still bet all they're worth on a sure thing.

Now I just have to figure out what sweet reward would tempt a psycho stalker-bully to come out of their hidey-hole.

In the past, I would have asked my dad for ideas. But he's in prison and not easy to contact. If Sam were here, I'd ask him. But he's not, and he's not taking my calls. Which I guess leaves Murphy. I'm still pretty irritated with him about the Carter thing, but he can be pretty creative when he wants to be.

I check my phone for the time: 9:49. Not too offensively late to make a call. Not that I mind being offensive.

I drop my feet and lean forward in my chair, resting my elbows on the desk as I scroll through my contacts list. I tap Murphy's name and press the call. But it's not Murphy who answers.

"Hi, Julep. This better be good," Bryn says.

Bryn often answers Murphy's phone for him. He thinks it's cute. I think it's nauseating.

"Frankly, I'm surprised you even picked up," I say.

"You have something on Skyla's stalker?"

"Not yet," I say as I reconsider telling her to put Murphy on the phone. Bryn might actually be the better person to ask about this. "I need some advice."

"That sweater you were wearing yesterday is hideous. You should burn it."

I rub the bridge of my nose. I did ask. I should know better by now, I really should.

"I need bait," I say, ignoring the malicious sweater attack. "Something juicy enough to convince Skyla's bully to crawl out from under their rock. Any ideas?"

"A really big jerk magnet."

"Come on. Seriously."

"Fine." Silence falls on her end of the line as she thinks. "There was that celebrity scandal last year—nude photos. But I don't know if we can get Skyla to pose nude . . ."

Nude photos. Of course. The con suddenly flares to

life in my tired brain, forming connections, cataloging resources, calculating odds. Now all I need is a hacker.

"Bryn, you're a genius," I say. "Put Murphy on the phone."

6

THE TALE

am

The next day, Roth is erasing the whiteboard when I walk in with another stack of blank quizzes, hot off the printer.

"Do you want me to leave these here or in your office?"

He looks at me, but he's distracted. He doesn't see me for a second or two. "Hmm? Oh, my office please."

I start to leave but stop just inside the door. "Sir?"

"Yes, Seward?"

"Have you heard about that mathematics conference coming up in Atlanta?"

"No. When is it?"

"Next Saturday. The focus is anabelian geometry. I read about your recent discovery online. Have you considered presenting at the conference?"

"Next Saturday?" He blinks, clearly recalibrating his

brain to the conversation. "No, no, no. I couldn't possibly be prepared by then."

"But there's a rumor that MIT—"

"No, I'm quite sure I'm not interested. But thank you for asking." He bustles past me into the hallway.

This is going to be harder than I thought.

Come on, Sam, obstacles are the fun part, Julep snarks in my head.

For you, maybe. For me, it just means more work.

I drop the stack of paper on Roth's desk, noticing a small, framed snapshot on his desk of himself and what I presume is his family—a woman with an Asian ethnicity and a boy who looked to be their son. Roth looks happy in the photo, about twenty pounds heavier and absent the wrinkles of care bracketing his mouth. Something happened between this photo and now, something bad.

I log the anomaly and leave the room. I still have two classes and a boatload of homework to do before casing the conference center. Hopefully, that at least goes smoothly. Fun part or not, I could do with a few fewer obstacles.

THE PUDDLES outside the Atlanta Buckhead Hotel and Conference Center reflect the blue from the restaurant patio lighting. Olson's dark hair and pale skin make her look like a black-haired Smurf in the blue glow.

"What are we doing here exactly?"

"A couple of things. We're checking out the space so we're prepped for the presentations. We're also testing the reservation. I hacked into their system and left a fake credit card number with a note that we prepaid. I want to make sure they don't have a backup system that I'm unaware of."

I fail to mention that I'm also keeping an eye on her for Walsh. Part of me is dying to ask her if she knows why he's even interested, but I don't want to creep her out before I know more. Maybe his interest is purely academic. My gut tells me it's more than that, though.

"How are you going to do all that?" She's officially gone from doubtful to a true believer. It would be sweet, if I weren't fifty-fifty on our chances of actually pulling this off.

"Ask."

She smiles and her dimple appears. I can't get over how different from Julep she is. Julep can play innocent, but she most definitely is not. Olson is like a newborn— all pink-tinged cheeks and awe-filled eyes. She's delighted by everything, even after someone she trusted took advantage of her. She's not at all the kind of person you'd expect at a military school.

"Welcome to the Buckhead Marriott," the polished desk clerk greets us. She sounds like a professional narrator. "How can I help you?"

"I'm the IT rep for Ammonite Symposia. I need to

check the sound and video equipment for the mathematics conference next week."

She taps the tablet mounted to the desk in front of her with robotic efficiency. The light from the screen illuminates her perfectly symmetrical features when she turns her professional smile back on me.

"Mr. Jackson?"

"That's me."

"I'll be happy to have someone escort you to the conference space as soon as I check your ID."

Olson twitches, but it's a slight twitch. Her expression doesn't falter. She's learning.

I hand the clerk the fake ID that Julep made me last September. I have to keep myself from sighing every time I use it. "Samuel L. Jackson" was her idea of a joke. Luckily, I don't have to use it often.

The clerk gives me the ID back after barely glancing at it. I probably could have handed her my actual ID and she wouldn't have noticed. She taps the screen a few more times.

"I've notified the concierge. He should be with you in a few moments."

"Thank you," I say with sincerity. So far, the customer service here has been stellar.

"So? Everything copacetic?" Olson asks as we move toward the conference rooms.

"Copacetic?"

"You know, in excellent order, satisfactory," she says.

"I'm familiar with the word. I'm just not sure I've ever heard anyone use it in actual conversation before."

She chucks me on the arm, though due to her combat training, it hurts more than she probably meant it to.

"Yes, everything's fine," I say, rubbing my arm.

The concierge leads us to the mezzanine level where the bulk of the conference rooms are situated. He shows us the room we'll be in, along with the audio/visual amenities. All the tech seems state-of-the-art and barely used. Shouldn't be a problem to hook up a laptop.

As we walk out, Olson shoots me a questioning look.

"What?"

"How did you get into the con artist biz? It's a strange sort of hobby."

"I met a girl in fourth grade who scammed me out of my lunch money for a month. I went hungry for a while, but I learned a valuable lesson."

"Don't make bets with your lunch money?"

"Don't make bets against Julep Dupree." I unlock the Volvo's doors as we walk up to it. "She needed a hench-man, and I needed a friend. I guess we both got we want-ed." Until I fell in love with her. So much for that valuable lesson.

We get in, and I start the engine.

"She taught you?"

"Some. But I got into the hacking side of it on my own. Her specialty was decoding people, mine was decoding networks."

"Was?" Her voice goes soft, as if she's afraid of poking a sore spot. And she's not wrong; it is a sore spot. But it's not like I can't talk about it.

"I should say 'is.' She's still in Chicago, and as far as I know still pulling cons."

"I'm probably prying, so feel free to tell me to shut the hell up if you don't want to answer my questions."

I shrug. "It's not a big secret."

"So why did you transfer to Giles?"

How do I even begin to answer that in a single sentence?

"Things got kind of intense. I needed a break."

"Military school is a break for you? Jeez. I'd hate to go through your version of intense."

I can't help but smile. "Fair enough."

She studies the dash for a moment before continuing. "My cousin told me some messed-up stuff about what went down with you. I thought he was making it up. Or at least exaggerating." I feel her gaze shift to my face. "He wasn't, was he?"

"Depends on what he told you, I guess. But yeah, probably not."

She looks out the window, turning the mood in the car heavy. Maybe it's time to change the focus. That's what Julep would do, right? Deflect.

"What about you? How did you end up at Giles?"

"Oh, no, you don't," she says, smiling at me. "My story

isn't nearly that interesting. Don't make me go after you, that's low."

I laugh. "Please. I need a little normal in my life. You'd be doing me a favor."

She shrugs. "My dad graduated from Giles. The end."

"Really? Mine, too."

"No way. What year?"

"Is that something I should know?"

She laughs. "I guess not."

The rest of the drive back to Giles passes too quickly, especially once we discover our mutual love of tactical role-playing games. She's surprising in more ways than one, it seems. And the transition from the slow strobe of streetlights to the blue-black of country roads adds to the intimacy, as if we've known each other forever.

When I pull up to her dorm to drop her off, the conversation dwindles as we try to figure out how to wrap it up. It occurs to me I've never had to navigate this kind of thing with Julep. She'd just say something flippant and get out.

"I had fun," Olson says, her eyes luminous in the glow from the landscape lighting.

"Me, too." I try not to let my surprise show.

I wait, the car idling, as she jogs up the cement steps and slips through the door to her dorm. But before I can move on to mine, I get a text from Pollack.

We have a problem.

"YOU MUST BE JOKING."

"I'm not, man. That's from the last hour alone."

Pollack turns his laptop to show me the screen, the blue glow adding an apocalyptical cast to our dimly lit dorm room. Neither of us wants to call attention to the fact that we're up past curfew. Our RA is pretty cool, but he gets in trouble if we get caught, so we try to keep it down when we flagrantly ignore school rules.

I study the web analytics for the symposium site, then toggle to our rapidly filling email inbox—requests for how to get tickets, how to order the materials, how to *volunteer*, for crying out loud.

"It's just a couple of math geeks showing a bunch of incomprehensible slides. It's not like it's SDCC or something." I scroll through the list of emails, assessing the damage.

"I guess people are really interested in the Alphabet Conjurer or whatever. Even the media wants an invite."

"It's the MIT rumor. It must be," I say.

"Well, whatever it is, I think you did your job a little too well."

"Thanks for the support, bro."

"Are we screwed?" he asks after a minute of tense silence.

My brain ticks through all the ramifications, all the

variables, all the possible outcomes. But in reality, nothing's broken yet.

"The amount of traffic we're getting isn't ideal. Too much light turned on the illusion will show its holes eventually," I say. "But for now we're okay. We just have to adapt."

"Can we hold out for another five days?"

I don't answer right away. I'm already adding a form to the website for ticket requests. It'll email requesters a ticket without charging their credit cards to keep up the illusion without adding *thief* to my rap sheet. The more people to witness Roth's downfall, the better, anyway. I answer the email from the local news station personally. A couple of the emails are acceptances from researchers I invited to present.

"I guess we'll see."

"Fabulous. Are we sure Roth is even coming?"

"I asked him and he said no."

"Seriously? Why?"

"He's only had a few days with the proof, and he's not ready to present it."

"Wasn't that the point of this whole symposium idea?"

"Yeah, but I thought the MIT carrot would be enough to get him to risk it. Apparently, it's not."

"Then how are you planning on getting him there?"

"The school president's going to pressure him into it."

"Since when?"

"Since we have the leverage to convince him it's a good

idea." I turn the laptop screen, with its climbing charts of website hits back to face Pollack.

"I NEED you to get me in to see President Brown."

I school my expression into neutrality as I wait at parade rest for Walsh's response. I'd rather chew off my own leg than ask Walsh for any favors, but the plan depends on it at this point. I keep my eyes fixed on the full size Gadsden flag he has framed on the wall behind his office desk. The *Don't Tread On Me* feels ironic, given he's the one doing the treading.

"Our arrangement does not preclude you from ritual forms of address, cadet. You will say *sir* when you speak to me. Every. Time."

"Yes, sir." I'd salute, but he'd pick up on the sarcasm instantly, and antagonizing him is not going to get me what I want.

"Cadets don't just get in to see the president. It breaches chain of command."

"I'm aware of that, sir. But if you want me to continue keeping an eye on Olson, I need to see the president."

"I can't see how one could possibly have anything to do with the other, Seward. Keeping an eye on Olson means keeping an eye on Olson."

Walsh leans against the edge of his desk, arms crossed in a posture of disdain. He's conveying in every way possible how much he detests me while also acting indifferent to whatever minimal threat I might pose to him or his position. I try not to acknowledge his paunchy, rough-shaven, slouchy dogmatism.

"We're working on a class project together, sir, and we need the president to sign off on the next stage of the assignment."

"What kind of assignment?"

"Statistics," I say with as much conviction as I can muster. I'm not currently enrolled in a statistics class, and if he knows my schedule, I'll have to talk fast to keep him from getting suspicious. But I picked statistics, because it's just boring and obtuse enough of a subject area that people's brains turn off when they hear the word. It's a solid choice, but my armpits are still sweating through my uniform. I'm not nearly as good a liar as Julep.

"Why does the president need to sign off on it?"

"Because it requires access to confidential demographic data that the school doesn't usually farm out to its students."

He narrows his eyes at me. "Fine. But once I get you an appointment with the president, I don't want to be involved again. You'll have to find some other way to fulfill your duties."

"Yes, sir," I say.

"Dismissed."

I get as far as the door before he stops me.

"Oh, and Seward."

I wait for whatever taunt he wants to fling at me, but damned if I'm going to 'sir' him again, threats of physical violence or no.

"I hear you've been getting closer with Olson lately."

That surprises me enough to glance back. "Isn't that what you want me to do?"

"Keeping an eye on her does not require long drives in the country. I want you both on campus at all times."

"Why do you care how I keep an eye on her as long as I'm doing it?"

"I care because she's my daughter. And I'll be dead in my grave before I let her date a—"

"Understood."

I walk out without permission.

Because she's my daughter.

I slam the door behind me.

7

THE TALE

*J*ulep

Unfortunately, it doesn't take longer than a school day for my shiny new outlook on the job to wear off. The dean seems to have caught on that something's up, because she was lurking not-so-covertly around every corner today. Plus, Skyla was out sick, which just makes me that much more cranky. I don't like the idea of her holing up alone when who knows what kind of nightmare is waiting to pounce.

"You'd better be right about this, Murphy," I mutter under my breath.

I kick an empty Solo cup out of my way as we navigate a musty commercial basement in Washington Heights, avoiding sticky patches and candy wrappers littering the floor as best we can by the cold light of clustering laptop screens and mobile devices. Murphy's leading the way, since he's actually been here before. Dani's trailing just behind us, her eyes scanning the room, though how she sees anything in this dismal cave is beyond me.

"Installing spyware I can do," Murphy says. "But if you want the honeypot, you need a real hacker."

"Like Sam," I mumble to myself.

Murphy shakes his head in the dim light. "There's nobody like Sam. He's the best I've ever seen. But this guy's almost as good."

I snort in disgust as I brush past a stained sofa with a couple making out to the four-four rhythm of the punishing techno beat. Almost everyone else is tapping keyboards and trash-talking each other in an equally techno language. The whole scene drives the spike of anger deeper. I shouldn't have to be here.

"What kind of name is Tog, anyway?" I say.

"You want the Tog?" interrupts a disembodied voice from behind a nearby monitor.

Murphy stops. "You know him?" he says, addressing the general direction the voice came from.

"Depends who's asking."

"We need help with a honeypot scam."

"That ain't saying who's asking."

I don't have time for this crap. I push Murphy aside and round the rickety table supporting the monitor.

"I'm asking." I pour all the HULK-SMASH surging through me into the two words.

"Damn, girl. That's all you had to say. Catholic school-girl wants me to do something . . . " Which he then follows up with a wolf whistle. Classy.

I size up the scrawny guy who just volunteered to be our guide. He's older than us, but not nearly as badass as he thinks he is. Oversized sunglasses. Enough bling to weigh down a rhino. He's lounging in a ripped chair, balancing a keyboard on one leg and a beer bottle on the other. I'm itching to knock that smirk off his face.

"What do you want with the Tog?"

"I have a proposition for him. Can you get him?"

"What's the payout?"

"That's between me and him."

He laughs. "Baby, you talking to the Tog right now."

I should have guessed someone named Tog would refer to himself in the third person. I just can't win for losing today.

His grin turns decidedly lecherous. "This proposition involve you paying me with that smoking body? Because I could be down with that."

I can feel Dani tensing behind me, which is just silly. I've faced zucchini scarier than this guy.

"This proposition involves me paying you with cash. Still interested?"

"Maybe."

I outline the basics of the scam Murphy and I cooked up last night. It's called the "honeypot" and has been used by hackers since there was a network for them to hack. It consists of a website on a controlled server that can fish out a visitor's IP address. In other words, I dangle some bait—nude photos of Skyla, in this case—and give the perpetrator a link. But instead of leading to nude photos, the link leads to an empty site that captures the perpetrator's IP address.

Once I have the IP address, I can use it to look up the physical address. And then I can have a little one-on-one with our new friend about etiquette and the proper way to treat a lady. There might be some thumbscrews involved. I like to be thorough.

After I've laid it out, Tog shrugs. "Doable. How much?"

"Three grand."

He purses his lips, pretending to mull it over. "I don't do white-hat. Could sully my rep."

"You'll bounce back."

This is why I hate bringing in contractors. Attitude, fair-weather loyalty. They're even worse for reliability than people who owe me favors. Plus, I have to pay them, which goes against every grifter grain in my body. But this is the only play we've got.

"You're lucky I have a weakness for spitfires with great legs. Otherwise, your mouth might try my patience. And I don't put up with mamas who try my patience."

I sense more than see his bouncers shifting position. The air in the room chills, though the keyboard clicks and mumbled conversations haven't lessened. Dani grips my upper arm, but I shake her off. I'm not leaving without a deal.

I rest my hands on either arm of his overstuffed chair and lean in, stopping an inch from his nose.

"What a coincidence. Because I have exactly zero tolerance for posers like you. But it so happens my far superior hacker is on vacay right now, so I'm in need of a temp. You don't want the job? Fine. I'll dig up your nearest competitor and give them the money and the bragging rights. And then I'll find your little sister—" I stroke his neck suggestively and wind one of the gold chains around my finger—"and tell her exactly what happened to all her costume jewelry."

Then I push against his chest to lever myself to standing. Murphy gapes at me. Dani's as stoic as always, but I can tell she's angry. Strangely, I'm not anymore. It's the grifter's high that comes from reading a mark and knowing exactly how to get him to do your bidding. Tog is a masochist in sadist's clothing. Deep down he wants someone to push him around. Give the mark what he wants . . .

"Six grand," Tog says, his voice husky.

I flash a version of his smirk back at him, hand on my hip bone in my best impression of a Bond girl. Then I turn and walk away.

"I'll be in touch," I call over my shoulder. Dani and Murphy follow me out.

Dani stews in silence the whole drive back to Bryn's house, which is where we picked up Murphy for our cracker-fishing expedition. I know she's mad, and I know why she's mad. But she's just going to have to get over it.

When I get out to let Murphy out of the Chevelle's backseat, he glances between Dani and me.

"Want me to drive you?" he asks.

It's a gallant offer, but I'm even less scared of Dani than I am of Tog, though not for the same reasons. Tog is all posturing and no teeth. Dani is the reverse. Her teeth are razor sharp, and she'd never give an enemy advanced warning. But I'm pretty sure she won't bite me, no matter how much I might deserve it.

"Nah. Thanks, though. I'll text you if I make it to the office."

He nods. "All right. Just try not to piss her off any more tonight."

"Come on, Murph. This is me we're talking about."

"Yeah, that's what I'm afraid of."

I push the passenger seat back into position and slide into it, shutting the door with the soft slam unique to muscle cars. Dani pulls away from the curb. She waits two whole minutes before laying into me.

"It makes me crazy when you do that," she says as she shifts gears.

"It makes me crazy when you act all overprotective. I was playing him, and it went perfectly."

"What if it had not gone as you planned? I counted

three guards at least. Not to mention his thirty acolytes. It was an unnecessary risk. You always gamble as if your life is worthless."

"Look, I didn't pick a job baking cupcakes. What I do is lousy with risk."

"You think I cannot tell when you are working and when you are being recklessly self-destructive?"

Okay, I might have gone a tiny bit off the rails back there, but I'm not confessing that to her.

"I wasn't being reckless. I needed his help and I got it."

"It is as if you are trying to punish yourself, or prove some sort of point."

"I'm not punishing myself." Though I deserve it and then some. "I'm just doing my job. And anyway, you're the one trying to prove something."

"What is that supposed to mean?" she growls.

My heart is hammering, and some part of my brain is screaming at me to shut my mouth. But I'm not famous for doing the right thing. I'm about to say something I know I'll regret. I say it anyway.

"You saved me from Petrov. Your promise to my dad is done, finito, over. But you're still here. And you still think it's your duty to protect me. Just so we're clear, I never asked you to."

She's silent for the rest of the trip to the Ballou, which to be fair is only a few minutes. But still. You could melt an iceberg with the heat scorching the car. I'm mad at her for being mad at me, but there's a significant amount of guilt churning in my gut as well when she pulls up to the door.

"You are right," she says, sounding resigned. "You did not ask. But I was not doing it for you."

"Dani—"

"Enough. It is your life to risk as you want. Just as it is my life to risk in your place."

"That's not—"

"All I am trying to say is that you do not have to suffer to earn forgiveness."

My breath seizes in my lungs like I've been tackled. She has no right to say that to me. No right and every right. She's the only friend I have left who's not just sticking around because she owes me a favor. How much longer until I drive her away, too? Or worse, get her killed?

I mumble something and bolt out of the car. I pass Yaji again without a word and climb the stairs to my office. When I get to my desk, my history book is still open to the textiles chapter. I put my head on my arms and cry like I haven't since Tyler died.

The next day after school, Bryn and Murphy and I reconvene at the Ballou office to lay the bait for the honeypot. Bryn and Murphy read over my shoulder as I type a private Facebook message from my own fake account to one of the bully accounts:

Psst. You really want to go after that skank Skyla? I found her boyfriend's phone and downloaded some naked pics. Check out this link...

"Can't you say boobs in there somewhere?" Murphy asks.

"No, I cannot. Perv."

"I'm just saying it would sweeten the pot."

"I think 'naked' is sweet enough." I paste in the link Tog sent me and send the message. "Now we just have to wait for the mark to click the link."

"What does the page say when the attacker clicks it?" Bryn asks.

"It just throws up an error message," Murphy says.

"You don't think that seems suspicious?"

"Doesn't matter," I say. "As soon as someone clicks the link, we'll have their IP address."

"And then what?"

"Then I look up who it belongs to and make them rue the day they ever heard of the Internet. The details depend on who it turns out to be."

"Why are we not telling Skyla about this?"

"She doesn't want to know who it is. Besides, she might accidentally let the plan slip to the wrong person."

I type a quick, insulting acknowledgment to Tog. It's our thing now—I take out all my pent-up, grief-fueled rage on him, and he reads the thank-you between the lines.

"How long will it take the attacker to click the link?"

"Hard to tell. It seems like the mark is posting every other day or so. It could be sooner than that, though, if they're set up to receive notification emails."

"Well, I hope it's worth the six thousand dollars you're going to bill her."

"Me too."

Bryn takes off to pick Skyla up at her boyfriend's place, leaving me and Murphy to sit and twiddle our thumbs.

"How'd your come-to-Jesus with Dani go?" Murphy asks from his desk a few minutes later.

I really don't want to answer that question. I'm still nursing a sore spot over the argument.

"Yeah, that's what I thought," he says.

I hide behind my laptop, answering emails, scheduling intakes, finishing up a homework assignment for government class.

"Murphy?" I say finally.

"Yeah?"

I stop typing, but I don't look at him.

"I'm glad you're—you know—here."

He doesn't answer, but the room is comfier than it has been in a while. He's not Sam, so I can't be sure he heard the apology I didn't quite say. But I feel a teeny tiny bit better. Now if only I could work stuff out with Dani. And Sam. I roll my eyes at myself. Might as well wish for the reappearances of Ralph and my mom while I'm at it.

I get an email from Tog. I assume it's an invoice for his

services, but when I open the message, I wave Murphy over.

"We've got a hit. The mark already tried the link."

While Murphy's crossing the distance to my desk, I highlight and copy the IP address Tog just sent me.

"Ready for the moment of truth?" I say.

"Always."

I paste the IP address into the search field on Whois.net and click the Search button. In seconds, the search engine returns a bunch of gobbledygook data that makes no sense to me. But in the middle of all the random netname, admin-C, source, and mnt-ref information is the pot of gold I've been waiting for. The mark's home address.

"Field trip?" I say.

After a quick jaunt in Murphy's van to residential Lincoln Park, we pull up to a Georgian three-story with immaculate lawns and a hedge separating it from the bourgeois sidewalk. Pretty much what I expected.

Murphy meets me on my side of the van. "What are you going to say? 'Who lives here and what do you have against Skyla Woodbridge?'"

"Yep. You coming?"

"Oh, I wouldn't miss it for all the panels at SDCC."

We walk up and ring the bell. A maid answers.

"May I speak with the head of the household?" I say, smiling pleasantly.

"Mr. Olson isn't home right now. He's at his son's base-ball game. May I give him a message?"

"I'm sorry. Did you say 'Olson'?"

The maid's eyes narrow. She's trying to figure out if she's done something wrong.

"As in Garrett Olson?" I continue.

Murphy looks as shocked as I feel.

Skyla's victimizer is her boyfriend.

8

THE SHUTOUT

am

I'm sitting in the mess hall hunched in front of my laptop when a pair of slim hands covers my eyes.

"Guess who?"

I pull away, breaking her light hold. "Cut it out, Olson. I'm not in the mood."

She plops into the seat next to me. "What bee crawled up your butt?"

"Your dad graduated from Giles?" I turn to glare at her.

The smile falls off her face. "He did."

"You neglected to mention the more relevant point that he still works here. You lied to me."

"I didn't lie to you," she says, angrily. "Not telling you everything isn't lying."

"It is. And I'm an expert on lying, so don't pull that

omission crap on me. How am I supposed to trust you now? If you lied about that, what else are you lying about?"

I get up and pace a few steps away from her, too aggravated to sit still.

"I'm not lying about any of it," she insists, getting to her feet as well. Her doe-eyes are wounded, as if I've just hit her with my car. "Roth stole my proof, I swear."

We're garnering some attention now from the other mess-hall inhabitants, but it's not enough to cool my self-righteous indignation. I'm pissed that she's related to that asshole. If she was raised by him, some part of her probably agrees with him, or at least sympathizes with him. It galls me to think I'm being played by a racist.

"It seems awfully convenient that you happen to ask the one person your dad wants to string up for help."

"Stop it." She blinks back tears. "I have nothing in common with that bastard. My mom divorced him five years ago, and so did I. That's why I go by her maiden name, Olson, instead of Walsh."

"But you still go to school here."

"Because it's a good school, the best in the state for math, and I get to go for free, because my dad works here. My mom could never afford a place like this."

"And what do you have to do for him in exchange for that favor?"

She pulls back as if struck. "Maybe you're the bastard."

Dude, chill, Julep says. *If Walsh were using her to get to you, he wouldn't have told you Olson was his daughter.*

Shut up, I tell her. I hear grumbling in my head but I ignore it.

"I'm out," I say. "I told you if you went off book one more time, I'd walk. Well, this is me walking."

"You can't. I need that proof back. It's only a few more days and—"

"It's not just a few more days." I try to keep a leash on my temper, but it's getting increasingly difficult. "It's my *life*. I'm not risking my place here for a person I don't even know."

She flinches as if struck and runs off. Good riddance. I sit back down and return to typing the cancellation message I'm about to email to all the registered conference attendees.

"What the hell was that?" Pollack asks, sliding into the seat Olson had initially taken.

"She lied."

"She's just a kid. She can't help who her dad is."

"Whose side are you on?"

"I'm on the side of the angels," he says, smiling. "Look, I get that you're pissed—"

"Her dad is a racist son of a—"

"So? Mine is a lazy deadbeat. Yours is a controlling jerk. That doesn't mean we're those things."

"She still lied."

"Yeah, but did it occur to you that maybe she lied because she likes you?"

My fingers falter mid-word. I hit the delete key pointedly a couple of times. "You're an idiot."

"You're the idiot. Anyone with eyes can see she admires you. Why would she want to admit that she's even remotely related to your arch nemesis?"

"That makes no sense."

Pollack leans forward. "What makes no sense is you jumping all over her like that. Your reaction was way over the top, dude."

It actually makes perfect sense, Julep says in my head.

I told you to shut up.

She's not Tyler, Sam.

And I'm not you.

No, you're a moron.

"You know what I think, Seward?" Pollack says.

"Why are you still here?"

He lets that roll off him. "I think you're scared. I think you're worried you can't pull this off, that you'll fail Olson and yourself and feel even more like a loser than you already do."

"You're wrong."

"Am I?" He stands and claps me on the shoulder before leaving.

I rub my ear. My cancellation email is ready to go. I slide the mouse pointer to the Send button and let it hover there for several seconds. Then with a heavy sigh I click the trash button instead.

I'M SITTING in the president's waiting room, tapping out and then deleting text apologies to Olson. Part of me thinks I'm still in the right about the lying thing. But Pollack's right, too. I turned on her for all the wrong reasons. So how do I explain that in a text?

I'm sorry. I send it and pocket the phone.

"Cadet Seward?" The heavyset secretary arches an eyebrow at me. "President Brown will see you now."

I stand quickly and go in, saluting the president after entering.

"At ease, cadet." President Brown gestures to a couple of seats near the window overlooking the quad. He leans on a cane as he rounds his desk on the other side of the room.

I step closer to offer assistance, but he waves me off.

"I got this retirement gift—" he taps his prosthetic leg with the tip of his cane "— leading a platoon in the Battle of Hue in '68. Never thought we'd make it out of that godforsaken swamp, but we did. And I swore I'd never lose another battle again. So I'll just walk on my own, thank you very much."

"Yes, sir." I back out of his way.

"Have a seat, Seward. They don't often let me talk to the students. I'm curious. Is the mess hall food as bad as the catered crap they serve at the fancy donor luncheons?"

I smile. "Just like Mama used to make, sir."

He laughs. "My mama must be a better cook than your mama, then."

He falls more than sits into the armchair across from the one he directed me to. I wait for him to settle his cane before I take my seat.

"What can I do for you, son? Everyone treating you all right?"

The way he's phrased the question paired with the glint in his eye leads me to believe he knows all about Walsh. For a moment, I struggle with the urge to admit everything—about Walsh, Roth, Olson, all of it. He'd probably be sympathetic, but sympathetic doesn't mean he'd help. He knows about Walsh and hasn't fired him, for one thing, so he probably only has so much power. And besides, without proof of the proof being stolen, I've got nothing.

"Actually, I'm hoping I can persuade you to help me convince Dr. Roth to present at an upcoming symposium."

I explain the details to President Brown, or at least, as many of the details as I can share without giving away the con. He listens with interest but stays silent for a minute or two after I finish, stroking his white, close-cropped beard in thought.

"This proof you're talking about. It could generate increased exposure for the school?"

I nod, though I don't mean it in the same way he's asking. Increased exposure, yes. He didn't specify positive exposure.

He thinks a minute more before gesturing to his desk. "Would you go get me my notepad and a pen, please? Upper left drawer."

I do as he asks and hand him the writing supplies. He dashes off a note, signing it with a brisk flourish. Then he gives it back to me.

"If you would do me another favor and deliver this note to Roth directly, I would much appreciate it. I believe he's working from home today. He lives in faculty housing, the green house on Patriot Lane."

"Of course, sir," I say.

It's a strange request. Why not send it through campus mail? I skim the note to see if there's some hint in it about why the president wants it personally delivered. But all it says is the president would appreciate if Roth would reconsider and present at the conference for the good of the school.

"Thank you for seeing me, sir." I tear the note off the notepad and then fold Dand pocket it.

"Thank you for calling my attention to the issue, Seward," he says and stands.

I salute and take my leave. The secretary barely looks up as I walk out. I check my phone but there's no answering text from Olson. Looks like I'm going to be making multiple house calls today.

I have to ask a couple of people for directions before finally tracking down Olson's room. Her message board says she's in class for another ten minutes, so I park myself on the front steps of the dorm to wait for her.

"Shouldn't you be in class?" Olson asks twelve minutes later.

I look up from the game I'm playing on my phone. "You didn't answer my text."

"So you skipped class to wait for me? That's interesting," she says in a flat tone that means it's anything but.

"I had already skipped class to talk to President Brown. I came here after that."

She's not glaring at me exactly, but her expression is wary.

"I just wanted to apologize again in person. I'm sorry I was such a jerk. I was mad, but you didn't deserve me going off on you."

"I appreciate that, I guess. And I get why you're upset. He's awful and abusive in general, and I'm sure he's been even worse to you. But I'm not him."

"Pollack said pretty much the same thing in your defense."

"So you're here because Pollack's making you apologize?"

"No. He just pointed out to me all the varying ways in which I'm an idiot."

She cracks a smile at that. A small smile, but it's something.

"In any case," I continue, taking a breath. "I didn't cancel the conference, on the chance that you still want to try to get your proof back."

"You didn't?" she asked, her smile starting to glimmer in her eyes.

"I didn't," I say, feeling both glad and unaccountably nervous all of a sudden. To distract her and myself, I hand her the note. "The good news is that I got some help from the president."

"Why didn't he just email Roth?" she asks after she's read it.

"He's like eighty years old. Maybe he's not comfortable with tech."

She rolls her eyes at me. "Please. My grandmother is practically an Apple superuser. When are you planning on delivering the note?"

"After I'm done groveling. I want him on the hook as soon as possible."

"Well, I don't know," she says, mischievously, tucking a lock of hair behind her ear and looking down demurely. "I think there's a fair amount of groveling still to be done."

"I could promise you my first born."

She snorts at me, grinning. "Isn't that supposed to be my line?"

"With AI, anything is possible these days."

"I suppose you're right, though I'd only accept if your first born happens to have your smile."

"Get a room!" someone catcalls from across the parking lot.

Olson doesn't look at them but flips the bird in the person's general direction, as she continues. "Make that your smile, and your XCOM2 AP."

"Temporary truce while I take that back to my lawyers?"

"Done," she says, then swirls off up the steps to her dorm. "Good luck!"

I SWING by the math department on my way to Roth's house. I have to invent some plausible reason for dropping in on him unannounced besides the note from the president. It'd be a dead giveaway that I had something to do with generating the note if delivering it was my only objective. Luckily, there's a stack of papers waiting outside his door for feedback, as well as a backlog of mail stuffing his campus mailbox. The TA angle is proving more useful than I thought it would be.

I find the green house without much trouble. Patriot Lane is a small side street directly behind the administrative building. The house is smaller than I'd have thought it would be for a tenured teacher. So different from St.

Agatha's, where most of the faculty lived in the wealthy suburbs.

The bell seems to be broken, so I try knocking. Within a few minutes, the door is opened by a kid of about twelve or so. I'm guessing the boy is Roth's son, but there's clearly something different about him. His gaze looks vacant, like he's not processing what he sees. And his movements are quiet and aimless, like a ghost's.

"Bobby? Who's at the door?" Dr. Roth comes into the hallway from a room at the back of the house. "Oh, Seward. What can I do for you?"

"I brought you some stuff from your office."

"That's nice. Come on in."

I walk past Roth Junior and into the stuffy entryway. Coats are piled in the corner behind the door, and as much of the house as I can see looks cluttered and dusty. Lived in, but not carefully cared for.

"Bobby, this is Sam Seward, my TA."

"Nice to meet you." I shift the stack of papers under one arm and offer the kid my hand.

He looks vaguely at me and then shuffles into the tiny living room without responding.

Dr. Roth's expression is a blend of affection and pain. "Please don't take offense. He has a rare genetic condition called neurofibromatosis—tumors that form along neural pathways and press on nerves. He has several in his brain, so he's lost a lot of cognitive function in the last few months."

He states it like a fact, but he makes no attempt to hide the undercurrent of sorrow.

"I'm sorry," I say. Because what else is there to say? It seems to be a theme I'm running with today.

"Nothing to be done," he says, smiling at me. "Let's see what you brought me."

I follow him into the room he'd emerged from—a poorly lit area that's actually smaller than my closet back home. There are papers piled on every surface, much as there are in his campus office. The man desperately needs a maid, or at least an assistant. Oh, wait. That's me.

The lone foray into the personal that's visible in the mess is a framed photo of a younger version of the woman I'd seen in the picture on Roth's classroom desk yesterday. I pick it up, curious where the woman is now.

"That's my wife," Roth says as he sorts through the packet of stuff I brought him. "She died last year of the same disease Bobby has. I should say that was my wife, shouldn't I? I'm still not used to saying that."

God, this guy just can't cut a break. I set the picture down quickly.

"What's this?" Roth picks up the fold-creased note from the president.

"It was in your mailbox." I wait for his eyes to shift to me in suspicion, but they don't. He sighs, his expression changing from sad to haggard.

I'm on the verge of running out of there, tail between my legs, when I happen to glance down and see a familiar composition book with Olson's name written in tight, square script on the cover. The title says ABC Conjecture. It would be so easy to steal back. Forget the symposium, the public humiliation, getting Roth fired. But there's no telling if he's made a copy. It would be easy for him to write it out in his own handwriting and claim Olson's was the stolen version since he'd already announced he'd discovered it.

There's no good solution here. Pursue justice and ruin a suffering man and his chronically ill son, or let him go and sacrifice Olson, an innocent and more importantly, a friend. Maybe I should tell her, let her decide. But I reject that thought almost as soon as I think it. I can't shy away from the responsibility for this. It's my guilt to bear. And suddenly I get Julep better than I ever have before, why she did what she did, as well as the full price she paid to do it. The price she still pays.

"Well, Seward, it looks like you get your wish. I'm going to present at the conference next week."

9

THE SHUTOUT

J*ulep*

We're winning. I think. It's hard to tell in baseball. There are runs and outs and strikes and fouls and everything is statisticized to within an inch of its life. I don't really do numbers. They're not as predictable as people.

Take Garrett for example. Easy to crack. Winning is everything to him, so the badger scam is the quickest way to tear him down. It's not even a scam really, since I have actual dirt on him. Murphy thinks I should wait to confront him, but I think the field is the perfect place. It'll remind him of all he stands to lose if I take this public.

After an interminable length of time, the game finally ends. Which means it's time for my game to start.

"Garrett." I keep my smile amiable as I approach.

Amiable like a piranha. "Great game. Good . . . what do you call it? Hustle? I'm not super into sports."

"Thanks." He looks shifty. And superhumanly attractive, with the artfully mussed black hair and the cheekbones. But mostly just shifty.

"Bet you're wondering why I'm here. Or maybe you're not. Maybe you have a pretty good guess."

"I don't, actually," he says. But he doesn't look confused. "Is Skyla okay?"

"See, that's the thing, Garrett. I think she could be okay. If she weren't dating a psychotic, abusive loser like you."

"What are you talking about?" Garrett's expression is a perfect hybrid of pissed off and confused.

"I'm talking about this." I hold up the Whois IP address entry I printed out. "Oops. Didn't think you'd get caught, did you? Well, you did."

"You think I posted all that crap about Skyla?" he says, disgusted. "I love her. Why would I do that?"

"I'm sure we could spend hours delving the deranged depths of your twisted psyche. But let's jump to the salient point, shall we?"

"I didn't—"

"Stop. Just stop. Delete your Facebook accounts. Otherwise, I'll be forced to take this issue to the dean. Do you really want something so scandalous on your permanent record? I can't imagine Cornell accepts many premed students convicted of harassment."

He snatches the paper out of my hands and skims it. "Just because someone used my IP address to post doesn't mean I did it. Someone could have cracked our wireless account. Someone could be trying to frame me."

"Why would someone want to frame you?"

"To throw suspicion off himself? I don't know. But it sure as hell wasn't me."

Much as I hate to admit it, he has a point. I can't prove it's him. It could be someone in his family. Or, less likely, somebody trying to frame him. If I get it wrong, the attacks will continue. And even if it is Garrett, as long as he has deniability, he can continue posting as long as he likes without repercussion.

"Where were you last night when the most recent posts went live?"

"I was at home." Aha! "With Skyla." Damn.

"All right, fine. You're off the hook for now. But you're still on my list. And the best way you can prove it's not you is by keeping this conversation to yourself. I don't want you tipping off the real attacker by letting them know we're on their trail."

"What about Skyla?"

"Not even her. She's already tied my hands enough with how I go about getting results. I don't want her micromanaging me on top of that."

"I meant is Skyla in danger? If someone's lurking outside my house using my IP address while she's inside, does that mean she's being stalked?"

I gape at him, stunned. I hadn't thought of that. If she is being actual-stalker stalked, that's a whole other ball game. For one thing, it means the mark has a wholly different agenda than I previously ascribed to them. If it's true, it changes everything.

"I don't know," I say. "But it's worth keeping a closer eye on her. Don't tell her, though. No point in panicking her over something we don't know for sure is happening."

He looks like he doesn't agree, but he nods anyway. "You'd better hurry. If this isn't resolved by the end of the week, I'm calling the police."

"That's probably a good idea," I admit. "Just tell me first, so I can get my people out of it. Not that what we're doing is illegal exactly, but some of them have reasons to avoid the police."

"Fair enough. And for what it's worth, I'm rooting for you. I don't want to put Sky through a police investigation if I don't have to. She's already been through so much."

"What do you mean?"

He's silent for a beat too long, like he's filtering. "It's not relevant. Just some awful stuff from her childhood."

"Everything is relevant until it isn't, Garrett. If you know something, you need to tell me."

His gaze drops and he shuffles uncomfortably. "I promised I wouldn't tell anyone. But if there's a chance she's being stalked..."

I wait patiently for him to come to terms with his

conscience. I'm so glad I don't really have one of those. Well, I have one, but it's pretty anemic.

Finally, he wrestles the words out. "Sky's parents are always touring without her. When she was younger, they hired a woman to be her caretaker while they were away."

I can already see where this is going.

"She abused Skyla. Horribly. But that was years ago. When her parents found out what was going on, they fired the woman on the spot and reported her to the police. And Sky hasn't seen or heard from the woman since. So it can't be related, can it?"

I would normally think not, if it happened years ago. But if the woman was reported to the police, she might be back for revenge.

"I wish I could say for sure it's not. It would be a stretch to assume it was related, since it happened years ago. But this case has been weird from the beginning. I'll just have to figure out how to get the mark to—" I stop myself from saying reveal themselves. Garrett is still a possibility, and I don't want to scare him off.

"To what?"

"To stop posting. Maybe it's time to get Facebook security to delete the accounts."

In reality, I have no intention of going to the authorities with this. We piqued the mark's interest with the tale of those pictures. It's time to move on to the shutout portion of the wire game. If only I knew how to translate the honeypot to something more concrete.

"Thanks, Garrett." I stuff my hands in my jacket pockets. "Don't be evil."

"I'll do my best."

I walk back to Murphy, who's been waiting in the stands this whole time.

"What did he say?" he asks when I reach him.

"He denied it, as you'd expect." I shiver, thinking about what else he revealed. "But I think we may have bigger problems."

"Like what?"

"Like trying to prove beyond a shadow of a doubt who's responsible. We can't prove anything with just an IP address. We need more. Otherwise, we're dead in the water."

Murphy sighs. "Unfortunately, 'dead' is starting to look like a literal possibility."

He hands me his phone with Facebook pulled up. It's one of the accounts attacking Skyla, the most recent post of which went live a minute ago:

Skyla-a-a-a, if you won't kill yourself, then I just might do it for you.

AFTER A LENGTHY, and annoying, brainstorming session with Tog and his team via video chat, we've come up with exactly nothing. Several ideas, each more elaborate and less likely to work than the last, streamed through the

Internet ether, clogging network connections with bytes of worthless junk.

Tog finally signs off, flipping me the bird for my parting snarky comment about his ridiculous chains choking off all the oxygen to his brain.

Murphy sighs. "You really ought to stop pissing off our best hacker."

"He's not our best hacker."

"No, he's our *only* hacker, thanks to your fight with Sam."

"It's not a fight," I snap back. "I'm not angry at him, and as far as I know he's not angry with me."

"Then why don't you call him?"

"Why don't *you* call him?"

"So we're in middle school now? I'm not playing go-between for you and Sam. Work it out, Julep. We need him."

I end the video chat with Murphy and lean back in my chair. I'm glad I have the office to myself right now. I still haven't heard from Dani, and it's making me angsty. I was probably too harsh on Tog. I was definitely too harsh on Murphy.

I'm sick to death of all my damage. I'm angry all the time, and whenever something irritates me even slightly, I snap. I used to have a sense of humor. I used to have a sense of self-preservation. Hell, Dani's probably right. Ever since the night I lost Tyler, and Sam, as well as my dad, my home, and my credibility, I've had this giant chip on my shoulder. Like wrapping myself in anger at the unfairness of it might somehow convince the universe to send them all back to me.

I look over at Murphy's empty desk chair, imagining Sam sitting there instead of Murphy. I can see him so clearly in my mind, even from the back. He's slouched over the keyboard, rubbing his ear while he's working out some obscure technical problem I wouldn't even know how to put into words, much less resolve. I blink to cut off the mental image. But the guilt polluting my chest is harder to alleviate.

It takes less than a second to dial his number. I hold my breath while it rings.

"Hey," he says.

Holy crap. He actually answered.

"Hey yourself." I am nothing if not articulate.

"I was just picking up the phone to call you."

I roll my eyes. "That's what they all say."

"No, really. I need your help. With a—" He pauses. "With a job."

Ouch. He's working without me? I guess I thought he just existed in limbo, doing military things while waiting for me to sort myself out. I didn't think he'd actually move on. Now I feel like dirt. And like an idiot. And like I need to get my act together if I'm going to salvage this conversation.

"What a coincidence. I need your help with a job, too."

"Oh."

What the hell am I doing? Why did I call him? About a job, no less. This is not how I wanted our first conversation post-mobpocalypse to go.

"Are you busy? If you're busy, I can call back," I say.

Cringe. I am so cringe.

"No, no. This is a good time. What do you need?"

So I explain about Skyla's problem. I even tell him about the abusive childhood caretaker. But mostly I talk about the shutout. About how I need to get the attacker to pop their head out of their hole so I can chop it off.

Sam listens with his usual attentiveness, asking all the right questions. And for a minute, it's like the last five months never happened. It's like he's my Sam and I'm his Julep and everything is as it was. And in that minute, my heart soars and burns to ash at the same time, though I absolutely lock my voice down to as measured and normal as I can make it.

"What about St. Agatha's computer lab?" he says when I'm done.

"What about it?"

"You have to log on to the computers to use them, right? It's easy enough to get those logs from the tech team if you can get the attacker there. Then just cross-check the login log with the site link you're using as the honeypot."

"But what would make them use a school computer instead of their own? It's not like we can disable all the computers in Chicago and force whoever it is to use the school's. And what if they're not a student?"

"Just change the error message on Tog's web page to something like 'This site is only accessible from the computer science lab at St. Agatha Preparatory School.' Maybe add a random string of numbers and letters to make it look more legit. If the harasser's not a St. Aggie's student, they'll let you know they can't get into the school, and you'll have at least ruled out ninety-nine percent of the possibilities."

I stare at my desk, floored by his brilliance. "That's—that's diabolical, Sam. And I mean that with the utmost respect."

He laughs. "I know."

I'm still reeling, my brain already spinning the details of the shutout. But something clicks over in my new-Julep psyche, reminding me other people have needs, too.

"What about you?" I say. "You said you needed help?"

He tells me about his job. It's another wire game. I almost comment on the strangeness of both of us running a wire game at the same time, when neither of us has ever successfully pulled one off before. But I don't. It's his turn to talk.

When he's done with his story, I sigh. "You can't con a selfless person, Sam."

"I know. But I have to do something. I can't just let Olson lose all her hard work. She'd be devastated."

I'm silent for several seconds, thinking. I know what I'd do, but it's nothing short of crossing a chasm and burning the bridge behind you as you go. I hate even suggesting he put himself at so much risk. I hate not being there to keep him safe. And yes, I realize what a hypocrite that makes me. But even if I ignore my own arguments, I can't help him. *He left.* He left me, and he's successfully moving on without me. I have to let him, if that's what he wants. It's what you do for someone you love, right? You let them be happy no matter how miserable it makes you.

I take a deep breath. "There is one thing you can do. But it's a big risk."

"Tell me."

So I do. I give him the only way out with any chance of him salvaging the situation. And as I do, I'm praying to every god I've ever heard of that my dicey solution doesn't take him down in the process.

"Are you sure?" he asks. And no wonder. It goes against everything I've ever told him. But I am sure it's his best shot, so . . .

"Yes."

"What do you think my chances of success are?"

"It depends on how you define success," I say, trying to be both positive and honest. "But if you mean everything working out to your benefit, I'd say fifty to one."

"Those are pretty crappy odds."

I choke back the words I want to say. *I'm coming. I'll fix it. Don't do anything without me.*

"Don't hate the player . . .," I say instead. Because at heart, I'm a jerk.

"Yeah, I know." He pauses, and I can practically hear him thinking. "Julep?"

"Yeah?" I say, my heart tangling in my vocal cords.

"I—" He doesn't finish, but he doesn't have to. I know what he's feeling.

"Me, too," I say. Then I end the call before I start crying again.

I set my phone down on the coffee-ringed desk, my thoughts whirling like desert-hot dust devils laced with jagged glass. Each gust nicks and burns me. So I still myself, ignoring the wind until my mind eventually empties. Then I pull my grifter grit from the deepest recesses of my soul, strapping it on like armor. And in the space of another breath, I'm ready to crush a villain.

10

THE SELFLESS CON

Sam

The day of the symposium dawns cold and bright. I know because I've already been up for two hours printing out all the badges, schedules, and signage to put the authenticity icing on this sham of a conference. I'd have done it last night, but I had another piece of the job to finish up.

Olson knocks and pokes her head into me and Pollack's room.

"Are you two decent? Oops, too late."

Pollack continues snoring in his junk-heap of a bed, one leg hanging over the edge. Olson walks over to his bed and hops onto it, pushing Pollack the rest of the way off, covers and all.

"What daffodil?" he protests sleepily before rolling up in his blanket on the floor and snoring again.

Olson looks at me expectantly. "Are we ready?"

I transfer one final file and smile back. "As we'll ever be."

It takes an hour to get out the door and to the hotel. Most of that time is spent convincing Pollack to orient himself along the vertical axis. Olson's nervous energy has yet to flag, though. She's almost annoyingly chipper.

"Sorry," she says, when I point it out. "It's my default mode for performance anxiety. I'll try to tone it down."

"Don't apologize. It's miles better than Slothman over there."

"Is he sleeping standing up?"

"It's his superpower."

She laughs, and the last vestiges of guilt I felt over tearing into her disappear. Whatever comes next, at least we're on the same page.

The hotel is bustling when we get there. Workers in starched uniforms are setting up chairs and swirling white and blue tablecloths over wide circles of plywood. The hotel conference coordinator stops by with an iPad and some paperwork to sign. We're hosting the conference in one of the hotels smaller auditoriums, which can be cordoned off into breakout rooms with accordion walls. We likely won't use them, but we close the walls anyway. It's an elite symposium with only enough tickets for a select few, after all. Closing off the extra rooms gives the space a more intimate feel. I turn off the overhead lights and dial up the dimmable wall sconces to help hide the fact that the room is mostly empty and very much lacking in the usual conference decor.

None of the attendees nor the presenters have arrived yet, but that's to be expected—we're early. We spend the final hour before go-time setting up the signs and tables, prepping the projectors, setting out the welcome packets, and redirecting trainspotters whose canceled conference we took the place of.

Pollack leaves to get coffee, and when he comes back with enough for all three of us, I take Olson's out of her hand and set it on the sign-in table.

"You can have it after the conference," I tease.

Our first presenter arrives at ten. After I show him into the presenter ready room, Olson makes herself scarce and Pollack takes a seat at the welcome table. Pollack's never had Roth as a teacher, so it's likely Roth won't recognize him. My job is to sit in the back of the room and run the projector.

As the attendees begin dribbling in and taking seats, I take out my phone. I'm nearly swamped by the urge to text Julep. Even though—knock on wood—the wire game seems to be coming together, I am not immune to the fact that I'm doing this without her. That this is the first time I'm pulling an entire con, start to finish, on my own. I can't help but feel the *wrongness* of it. She should be here. Or I should be there. I'm not sure which.

It gets so bad that I scroll to her name in my contacts list just to see it.

Jesus, I'm pathetic.

"I believe I made it clear that I didn't want you leaving campus with my daughter, Seward."

I look up from my phone to see Walsh looming over me. I'm too keyed up to be intimidated, though. Besides, what can he do to me here?

"We had a previously agreed upon engagement. Sir."

"Well, I don't allow disobedience without consequence, Seward. You can expect your penalty when you return to school."

Whatever. It's not like I've never been disciplined before. I was in a shootout with the mob. I think I can survive Walsh's goons. And if everything goes according to plan, I may not have to.

"If you would take your seat, sir. The presentations are about to start." I smile at him. He narrows his eyes but moves away to find a seat on the opposite side of the room.

I dim the lights with my phone and queue up the first presentation. One of the other presenters, who agreed to be our MC, gives a brief introduction of the speaker. The speaker takes the stage and walks us through his presentation.

I use the time to tie up a few loose ends on the hacking side of things, as well as the more legitimate parts of the plan. I check my email during a particularly boring stretch about prime factors of the sum of a and b. The shiny new message waiting there makes me smile. Maybe I might actually pull this off.

Then Pollack sends me a text.

We have a problem.

I text back. *I'm going to strike that phrase from your vocabulary. Permanently.*

Our plan is going down the crapper. How's that?

"WHAT DO WE DO?" Olson asks, tugging her braid. This is the second time in less than a week I've nearly made her cry. What does that say about me?

"We are not going to panic."

"How can you not be panicking? Roth cancelled. He called the front desk and cancelled. He's not coming. He's not going to bring my proof. All of this was for nothing."

She's dangerously close to flailing. I grab her hand to get her attention.

"Roth's been against the conference since the beginning. Do you really think I wouldn't have a contingency plan?"

Hope returns to her expression. "You have a contingency plan?"

"Olson, this is what I do. Give me a little credit."

To be clear, I don't have a contingency plan, but I'm sure as hell not telling her that.

"What is the contingency plan?"

"I'll take care of it. But I need you to stay here and keep the conference running. Can you do that?"

She scoffs at me. "I'm not completely helpless," she says. "I can't vouch for Pollack, but I have some skills."

"I never doubted it, skipper."

She brightens at that, though I have no idea why.

"You're in charge of this fiasco till I get back. Don't let the nerds eat each other alive—you know how they get at these things. I'll be back as soon as I can."

"Okay," she says. Then she kisses me. On the cheek, but still.

"I—um." I clear my throat. "Take over for Pollack, will you, so he doesn't spill Coke all over my laptop?"

She nods, blushing, and slips into the auditorium.

I swallow hard. I can't think about Olson right now, though. I have no idea what to say to get Roth to ignore his own common sense and present something he barely understands to a roomful of experts. I'd read him poorly. He isn't ambitious, conniving, and disreputable. He's just trying to survive each day. And not for himself but for his son. He's not a bad guy. Okay, he's not that bad a guy.

The problem is incentive. Julep says that conning a greedy man is easy, conning a smart man is trickier, and conning an honest man is the hardest of all. But conning a selfless man is simply impossible.

Any bright ideas? I ask the Julep in my head.

Beats the heck out of me. I'm just a figment of your imagination.

I sigh and pull out my phone. I haven't talked to the real Julep since the night at the warehouse. But I need her advice. I've grifted myself into a corner, and she's the only one I trust to pull me out.

But just as I'm about to call her, my phone vibrates and her face lights up the screen. I tap to answer.

"Hey."

I am nothing if not articulate.

"Hey yourself," she says back. And hearing her voice is like a river washing over a dry creek bed, soothing the cracked earth with life. But at the same time, it's like I'm on the edge, watching the water run by. Grateful, but. . . apart from it somehow.

"I was just picking up the phone to call you."

"That's what they all say."

"No, really. I need your help. With a—" It suddenly occurs to me that she may not react well to the news that I'm branching out on my own. But the thought only gives me slight pause. If she hasn't guessed already, she won't be that surprised. "With a job."

"What a coincidence. I need your help with a job, too."

"Oh." I'm somewhat deflated that she called looking for help, never mind that I was just about to do the same thing.

"Are you busy? If you're busy, I can call back," she says.

"No, no. This is a good time." Actually it's not, but I'm on a roll. "What do you need?"

She fills me in on the honeypot scam, and I'm shocked she's running a wire game at the same time as me. What are the odds of that happening? In any case, I point out a side door she hadn't considered, and when I've explained it, she calls me diabolical. It's pretty much the nicest thing she's ever said to me.

"What about you? You said you needed help?" she says.

As quickly as possible, I tell her everything. Well, everything related to the con. I don't mention the cheek kiss or the conversations I've been having in my head with pretend-Julep. Despite popular opinion, I'm not an idiot.

She sighs. "You can't con a selfless person, Sam."

"I know. But I have to do something. I can't just let Olson lose all her hard work. She'd be devastated."

Julep is silent for a few long seconds. I wish I could read her mind, but then I've wished that since we were twelve.

"There is one thing you can do," she says. "But it's a big risk."

"Tell me."

Her advice is nothing short of a nuclear option. It's even more absurd than I expected, and I expected epic levels of unhinged, given. . . well. . . Julep. Not to mention, it's almost guaranteed to fail. But if she's suggesting it, then there are no better options.

"Are you sure?" I ask, but I don't have to. She wouldn't tell me unless she were.

"Yes."

"What do you think my chances of success are?"

"It depends on how you define success. But if you mean everything working out to your benefit, I'd say fifty to one."

"Those are pretty crappy odds."

"Don't hate the player . . ."

"Yeah, I know." I rub my ear, thinking. "Julep?"

"Yeah?"

"I—" I don't know what I'm trying to say, but it has to do with the cactus that's permanently lodged itself in my ribcage, right up next to my heart.

"Me, too," she says and then hangs up.

I think about that cactus all the way to Roth's house.

I KNOCK on the door and let myself in. Roth is in the living room, sitting next to his son on the couch. He has one arm around Bobby. The other cradles Olson's composition book.

He looks up when I sit in the chair opposite the couch.

"You're not really my TA, are you?" he says, his expression resigned.

I shake my head. He bows his.

"How long has he known?" he asks.

"Who?"

"The president."

"He doesn't know," I answer honestly. "Yet."

"Then you're here to blackmail me?" He laughs without humor. "Take whatever you want. What you see is what I have."

Bobby stirs, probably reacting to his father's distress. I don't want this to go badly for him. I don't want it to go badly for anyone. Okay, maybe I want it to go badly for Walsh, but I want everyone else to end up at least no worse off than they are now.

"I'm not here to blackmail you, Dr. Roth."

He rubs his forehead with a shaky hand. "I'm sorry. I'm sorry, I. . . I didn't want to hurt anybody. But I need this position. I can't lose my healthcare benefits, not with Bobby as sick as he is. It's the only job I have the skills for that is flexible enough to let me take care of him. But I need to publish or I lose credibility in my field. And I haven't been able to concentrate on anything but Bobby. I really didn't mean any harm. You'll tell her that for me, won't you?"

"Why don't you tell her yourself?"

He winces. "I can't."

"I think you can." I lean forward in my seat. "I think you have to." His face crumples. I get up and take the composition book from him.

"I can't promise you anything other than you won't regret it," I say, remembering the look on Julep's face when she showed me the hundred haunted girls she'd sacrificed her freedom for.

When he gets to his feet, I hand him back the book.

"Trust me."

11

THE STING

J *ulep*

It's D-day, and the only ones who know it are me, Tog, Murphy, and the mark. I contacted Tog last night after my talk with Sam about changing the error message. I also sent another Facebook message to the mark saying that the web link I'd sent before was broken, that I'd fixed it and it was set to expire by noon today. The classic shutout: a ticking clock. The bait is ten times more tempting if it's a limited-time offer. But it's risky. I won't be able to use the same trick on the mark twice. Hopefully, I won't have to.

I'm not concerned about the mark at the moment, though. I'm standing outside a nondescript apartment building in Chicago's March drizzle, waiting for a chance to make amends. The rain complements my mood, so I don't mind it. And this time I've got an umbrella.

"What are you doing here?" Dani asks as she walks up to me.

It's a fair question. I've been loitering outside her apartment for twenty minutes now waiting for her to come out, and I'm skipping school to do it.

"It's raining," I say.

"Is it."

I hand her the umbrella, and she takes it without moving her gaze from mine.

"I'm not really any good at this," I say, hating how awkward I feel.

She's not smiling, but she's not scowling either. She seems curious to see where I'm headed with this. Well, so am I. I didn't exactly come with a speech prepared.

"I need you. I mean, I know that you already know I need you. But the part you don't know is that I know that I need you. I know it. I don't say it. And I keep myself from asking for your help because I— because I'm afraid of needing you. Or rather, of admitting I need you and then losing you, too. So I don't say it. But I do know it."

Dani's expression turns completely unreadable. Her guard is so good that I feel like I'm always knocking at the door with her, when, with most other people, I just open the door and waltz right in.

"Dani . . . " I feel like I should kneel or something, which is just weird. "Will you help me?" Pretty sure there should be a *please* in there somewhere. "Please?"

She doesn't answer right away, so I keep going like an

idiot. "I—I mean, obviously you've been helping me all along, and I'm grateful. I'm just officially, you know, asking —for myself. Ugh, damn it, I'm messing it all up."

She smiles, shaking her head, and hands me the umbrella. "Get in the car. I will drive you to school."

BY 11:54, I'm tapping my foot and checking my phone every two seconds. Ms. Shirley knows something's up. For one thing, I'm actually sitting in my chair instead of meandering the halls like I usually do during study hall. For another, my eyes are permanently glued to the clock above her desk.

Promptly at 11:55, the bell rings for fourth period. Everyone files out except for me and Ms. Shirley. There's no fourth-period class in the computer lab, so I slip into the back and wait. If anything's going to happen, it'll be in the next five minutes.

Students do trickle in to check their email and such in between periods, so there's enough cover for Skyla's attacker to risk exposure if the lure of the pictures is tempting enough. I'm not sure what I'll do if this doesn't work. And it's not out of the realm of possibility for it to fail miserably—the attacker not being connected to St. Agatha's and therefore not being able to access the computer lab being the least worst way it could go wrong. The wire game is a difficult con under the best of circumstances, and these circumstances are more like a sack of fireworks than circumstances.

Murphy strolls in and finds me in the back. He nods when he sits in the chair next to mine, but he doesn't say anything. We're both strung as tight as piano wire.

The door opens whisper soft. I see Ms. Shirley look up and down again. A student, then. Someone she's used to seeing. But I can't tell who it is right away. The monitors are blocking my view.

Then I see her. And it's like taking a wrecking ball between the eyes.

Skyla.

My first thought is she's going to ruin everything. Her attacker's not going to show up if she's sitting right in the middle of the room.

My second thought is much worse.

Murphy starts to stand, but I clamp my hand on his arm, stopping him with a look. He sinks back into his chair without a sound.

Something about this isn't right. Something about this job has been irking me from the beginning.

I'm not strong like you or Bryn.

We watch as she logs into a computer, as she pulls up the Facebook account, as she navigates to the message I sent with the honeypot URL, as she clicks the link that leads to nowhere. We watch as she tries to destroy herself.

"What the hell?" Murphy murmurs.

I stand and walk slowly to Skyla. She's facing away

from me, so she doesn't see me at first. When she does finally catch sight of me, she jumps up and makes a break for the door. Murphy blocks her exit, and she whirls to face me.

"Hey, what's going on?" Ms. Shirley says from her desk.

"She deserves it," Skyla says. "She's a conniving whore. She doesn't deserve him."

I keep my voice as calm and nonthreatening as possible. "Who deserves it?"

"You can't make me say her name. I know your tricks."

Her eyes are wild, and . . . different. It's like she's seeing me and not seeing me at the same time. She recognizes me, but she's not acting like Skyla.

"Please, tell me. Who deserves it? Who are you talking about?"

Murphy's face is ashen, and I'm sure mine is just as bloodless. Something is very, very wrong here.

"She's just using him. She's a bad, bad girl. She needs to be locked in the dark. She needs to die."

She pulls a razor from her bag and slashes at us with it. Murphy and I jump back. She manages to snag Murphy's forearm anyway. A trickle of blood drips down to his hand, but he ignores it. Instead he leaps forward, grabbing her wrist. But then Ms. Shirley hurtles into the fray and hijacks the razor from Skyla's grip.

Skyla passes out in Ms. Shirley's arms. Sort of. Her

eyes are still open, but she doesn't seem to be seeing any of us.

"You can let go, Murphy," Ms. Shirley says. "Can you please get the dean?"

He leaves, and I stand there shaking like a leaf, trapped in visions of somebody else's blood, somebody else's vacant eyes staring up at me.

"Julep." The emphasis in Ms. Shirley's voice leads me to believe she's said it more than once.

"Yes?"

"Are you okay?"

I shake my head. "I'm fine."

"Please have a seat. And breathe for me, okay?"

I do as she says, though I have no conscious thought of locating a chair.

"What happened?" she asks.

I tell her the whole story from front to back. I don't leave out anything. All the names, dates, and places. I'll have to tell it again to the dean, and probably the police officers, and maybe some kind of social worker.

But I actually don't mind. This is beyond my ability to help. I can't fix this. I can't fix this for her. I'm going to have to give her a refund.

The incongruous thought sparks a laugh. It's small and hysterical, and nothing about this situation is funny, but it comes out anyway. And to be honest, I much prefer it to the tears I can feel burning like thermite in the back of my throat.

The rest of the day is a blur of interviews, debriefings, questions, and answers that go around and around and nowhere at the same time. Murphy comes back to help me give an official statement, as the school nurse patches up the cut from the razor blade. But all I can think during the debrief is that she was right in front of me the whole time, begging for me to help her. And I didn't hear it. I wasn't listening.

When Mike finally manages to pry me free from the chaos, he drives me back to his house in silence.

"We'll talk in the morning," is the only thing he says to me, for which I'm profoundly grateful. He gets me, I'll give him that.

But before I crawl into bed, knowing the terrible nightmares I'm going to have, I kneel on the floor and offer up the first real prayer I've ever said.

...Our Father, I pray that through Your intercession of St. Nicholas, You will protect the children...

THE WHOLE SCHOOL is still on fire with gossip Monday morning. A lot of heads are turned toward me, but nobody's asking me anything. I almost skipped, but when Dani showed up this morning to drive me, I was too grateful to see her to play sick.

Bryn looks wrecked and Murphy has hardly left her side all day. He walks her to and from all her classes, which is sweet. I actually try to think of a person who owes me a favor that I like enough to force them to walk me to and from all my classes, but I can't think of anyone. So I walk the halls alone.

When I saw Bryn before school, she told me about the journals they found in Skyla's room. Most of them were filled with diary entries you'd expect from a well-adjusted high-school girl. But there were a few, squirreled away under a loose floorboard that contained wild, vitriolic entries, that started well over a year ago.

I'm not sure how no one's caught on before now, but Bryn's guess is that falling in love with and dating Garrett had forced Skyla's trauma from the abuse she'd suffered as a child to the surface. Not that Skyla hadn't had mental health concerns from the trauma all along, but until that point, she'd managed to repress the worst of it without her parents or therapists or even herself knowing about it.

Then when she fell in love with Garrett, and felt his love for her, it triggered the guilt and shame she'd internalized from her childhood abuser's verbal attacks about how she was unlovable and unworthy and unclean. Over time, it built to such a degree that it gained a measure of control over her. Oddly, Skyla has no memory of the times when she's not in the driver's seat. She had no idea the alternate diaries even existed until her case worker found them and showed them to her.

The small but significant silver-lining in all of it is that Garrett is showing up for her like no one else in her life ever has. He's staying with her in the hospital until her parents show up. If they show up.

After school, Murphy and Bryn meet me in the student parking lot. Murphy leaves Bryn in my care while he wraps up some loose ends with the tech club. He's agreed to disable the spyware for me, minus the one on the dean's computer, so I can sleep at least a little better at night.

"How are you holding up?" I ask Bryn as Murphy heads off toward the computer lab. Her eyes trail after him in a bereft sort of way.

"I'm all right," she says without looking at me. "I'm just worried about Skyla."

"I am, too," I say.

She arches an eyebrow at me, finally turning her head my direction.

I glower back, though not as heatedly as I might under normal circumstances. "She may not be my BFF, but I care about my clients' wellbeing."

"You saying that is not the strange part," Bryn says. "The strange part is that I believe you."

I watch classmates chatting around their cars, joking and bickering and bonding like nothing can hurt them. Like Skyla isn't suffering. Like Tyler isn't dead.

"What happens now?" I ask.

Bryn fidgets with her bag strap, shifting her weight uncertainly. "Now she goes through a ton of tests and a lot of therapy. But she'll have the best help money can buy."

"The best help would be her parents' actually being there for her," I point out.

"Like I said. The best help money can buy."

We stand in glum silence for a moment, and I think of last October and all the ways we sabotage ourselves and the people we love.

"Do you think we're doomed to repeat our parents' mistakes?" I ask out of nowhere. I'm not the heart-to-heart type, and even if I were, I wouldn't normally choose Bryn of all people to open up to.

To her credit, Bryn doesn't immediately smack me down. She actually thinks about her response before answering, which just shows how distraught she is.

"I think we're doomed to make our own mistakes, whether they relate to our parents or not."

"Great," I say. "So we're doomed *and* it's our fault."

She actually smiles at me. A half of one, but I'll take it. It's a rare feat to make Bryn smile.

"Want a coffee?" I ask.

"You paying?" Bryn quips back. She's already starting to sound more like her usual self.

I start moseying in the direction of the Ballou. "Well, I'm officially broke now, since I refunded Skyla's retainer, and Tog's still expecting his fee."

Bryn bumps me with her shoulder in an almost friendly way. "You did make the posts stop," she says quietly. And I nearly trip over the implied thank-you.

To distract myself from the surreal feeling of Bryn

being nice to me, I change topics. "I probably owe Garrett an apology. I called him a psychotic, abusive loser."

She rolls her eyes. "He'll get over it. Besides, he has bigger problems right now."

I push back thoughts of all the people who have left me when I say, "Skyla's lucky to have him."

Bryn shrugs. "He loves her," she says, as if it's that simple.

I shake my head. "People say 'love' like it's the answer to every question, but love is just another wire game. It sets you up with a tale about something that doesn't exist. Then it shuts you out, just to make you crave it more. The second you go all in, it takes you for everything you're worth, leaving you with nothing."

Bryn stops walking and turns a sulfuric glare on me. "Bullshit," she says.

I blink at her in surprise. I think it's the first time I've ever heard her swear.

She tosses her head. "You think because you can manipulate people that you know everything there is to know about love?"

I never said I knew everything about anything, but she's waiting for an answer.

"Maybe I don't know everything about love," I admit. "But I do know that it usually causes the problems I end up having to fix." Like hyper-paranoid fiancés, for example. Or my own ruined heart.

Bryn's expression morphs into something that looks

suspiciously like pity. But she lowers her voice so I'll listen.

"Murphy buys me mint-chocolate-chip-flavored gum every time he sees it, because I once said I liked it. I have an entire desk drawer at home full of gum now. I open it sometimes just to look at the piles and piles of gum he's given me over the last few months. Because I know what love is, Julep Dupree. And it's not some two-bit con."

She storms up to the door of the Ballou, her heels clicking on the pavement. She grabs the handle but turns back to me before pulling it.

"Maybe Tyler's death made you jagged-edged and bitter. But love didn't kill him just to piss you off. And if you really believe that crap you just said, then you didn't care about him at all."

She walks into the Ballou without me, letting the door swing closed behind her. I stand there awhile and think about Murphy's happily ever after and how I was wrong about his broken heart.

If I was wrong about that, then perhaps I'm wrong about other things.

And if I can be wrong about things, then perhaps there's hope for me yet.

12

THE STING

Sam

When we get back to the conference, Roth and I steal into the back of the darkened auditorium. A local media affiliate is filming the stage. The reporter, or more likely intern, is staring at his nails, clearly bored. The speaker wraps up his presentation on something so indecipherable that it doesn't sound like he's speaking English. The MC returns to the stage and introduces Dr. Roth.

Roth takes a breath and walks with purpose to the stage. He climbs the side stairs and walks to the center. He then stands behind the lectern like he was born to it. He takes a moment before opening his presentation. I should be worried about what he's going to say. He could do anything with that spotlight. But I'm not worried. I feel it —the perfect synergy of all the cogs fitting together the way they were meant to. As if I'd planned it this way from the beginning, even though I really didn't.

Julep calls it the Roman principle, after the keystone in Roman engineering. The keystone holds all the other stones in an arch in place, though there's no obvious reason why it should. None of the other stones are glued together. Something about the keystone just magically keeps the other stones from falling. The con artist's job is to keep the other stones together until the keystone settles into place on its own.

When she told me this, I immediately pointed out that the Roman Empire fell. She then painstakingly explained that the Romans were the grifters and the arches were the jobs—the Romans came and went, but the aqueducts were still in use two thousand years later. I believe I then called it a ridiculous, convoluted metaphor, to which she rolled her eyes and said that the comparison *literally* held water.

I smile at the memory. And though the cactus is still there under my ribs, I don't mind it as much. It's a bitch of an albatross, but it's mine.

I scan the crowd for Olson. She's sitting by the projector. She gives me a thumbs-up when she catches my gaze. I nod back, though I don't think she's prepared for what's about to happen. She probably won't like it, but there's nothing to be done. I'll have to apologize—again—later.

"The most rewarding aspect of my job is the opportunity to bask in the unadulterated brilliance of young minds. It's been said before, but it's the second truest theorem of life I've ever come to understand: I learn more from them than they do from me. The proof is undeniable. In this case, I mean that in the most literal sense.

"One of my students recently reminded me that if you want a good education, you need to study with the best. Well, I have had the great privilege of studying with the best young mind in mathematics today. Her work on Mochizuki's ABC conjecture is groundbreaking. But I'll let her show it to you herself. Please welcome Ms. Katherine Olson."

The applause is scattered and unsure. None of the attendees quite know what to make of this development. Half of them probably think it's a joke. But at least the reporter has woken up. He's scribbling notes in a flurry. I could give him a story. I slide my fingers over my phone, thinking of the contingency plan I'd recorded not an hour ago that I now wouldn't need to use.

Olson's eyes are huge as she looks to me for a cue. I make a shooing gesture at her. She shakes her head in disbelief, seeming to be more in shock than mad. Which is a good sign . . . I think.

As she takes the stage, I sense a malevolent presence just behind me. I turn to see an irritated Walsh.

"What is this about, Seward?"

"What's that, Walsh? No appreciation for your daughter's impending fame?"

"I ordered you to watch her, not make a fool out of her."

"I'm not making a fool out of her. She's presenting her proof to a roomful of academics."

"You end this farce of a symposium right now before I call your uppity father and—"

"That's quite enough, Lieutenant Walsh."

Walsh jumps as President Brown's voice joins the conversation. "President—"

"I find your choice of descriptors interesting. But what I find even more interesting are the files I found on the school network implicating you in some sort of false symposium scandal. My counterpart at MIT is very put out that his school's name has been linked to an event it had no knowledge of."

"Sir, I had nothing to do with this."

"Really? Then why is your name listed as the originator of the files used to build the website for the symposium? Also, there's this rather compelling video of you confessing to all sorts of things."

"No. That's not possible."

"That's what I would have said two hours ago. Sadly, the proof speaks for itself."

I take that as my cue to duck out of the conversation. With any luck, the beefy guys flanking the president will be relieving Walsh of his duties before the end of the conference.

I'm not sure how Walsh's forced resignation will affect

Olson's ability to stay on at Giles, but I'm not too concerned about it. I can't imagine President Brown will have trouble digging up a scholarship for a celebrity math genius. And if he can't work it out, plenty of other schools would throw themselves at her feet now, if she so much as glances in their direction.

I find Pollack at the laptop, cheerfully checking his Facebook feed while Olson waxes poetic about her discovery. The projector is still attached, but I don't think anyone is paying the screen any attention. Everyone's eyes are drawn to Olson like rare-earth magnets. Even mine. She's glowing up there, Roth standing a respectful, supportive distance behind her. Every syllable out of her mouth is magic. Roth may have been born to lecture, but Olson was born to inspire.

When she finishes, the crowd is no longer uncertain in its applause. The auditorium reverberates with an ocean of sound, and nearly every attendee has risen to his or her feet. She doesn't know what to do with the praise, so she clutches her composition book to her chest and grins from ear to ear. I can't help grinning, too. Even Roth is clapping, though his life is crumbling around him because of his decision to come clean.

I know it will be a long wait when nearly half the audience rushes the stage to introduce themselves and congratulate her. She has a long way to go before her proof is officially verified and corroborated, but she's hot stuff right now, and people know history in the making when they hear it.

Pollack and I spend the first hour breaking down the chairs, though technically the hotel staff should take care of it. I just need something to do. There's still one loose end to tie up, and I'd like to do it before I collapse.

"Hey, buddy," Pollack says, stacking the last chair against the wall. "I'm toast. Mind if I hitch a ride back with the president's entourage?"

"Not at all. Thanks, Pollack."

"Any time." Pollack leaves, and I sink into the one remaining seat in the middle of the room, waiting for the last stragglers to leave the stage. Olson looks as tired as I feel but also radiant.

When the final admirer departs, she bounces off the stage and run-hugs me. Then lets go as fast and twirls around a few times. Roth follows, hanging back. Since he's the one I have unfinished business with, I get up from my seat, ignoring the Disney math-genius princess, and hand him a piece of paper I'd printed at the hotel business center while I waited for them to finish with their fans.

"What's this?" Roth asks.

"It's a choice," I say, letting him read the message for himself.

"I don't understand. It says I have an interview at the Neurofibromatosis Network in Illinois next week."

"I took the liberty of sending out the curriculum vitae you submitted as part of your presenter application. I found a few places I thought would appreciate your skills while giving you what you need to provide for your son. Of course, you could stay at Giles, but in case the president gives you a hard time about the proof. . ."

"But how. . . why. . . ?" he stammers.

"You've been planning this from the start, you jackass," Olson says, shoving me. But her eyes are shining and she doesn't seem mad. "How did you do this? How did you know it would all work out like this?"

Easy—I didn't.

"I'm a professional," I say instead. She shoves me again.

THE DRIVE back to Giles is as nice as the one several nights ago was. I'm reluctant for our easy camaraderie to end. Olson is a whirlwind of happy, and it's hard not to be sucked into her vortex of bliss. I'm not sure why I'm resisting. And even as I think that, my resistance slips that much more.

"Want to go for a walk?" Olson asks when we pull up to her dorm.

"Sure."

I park the car, and we head for the quad. A paved path curls around simple landscaping—trees, mulch, grass, a berm here and there for variety. The sun is setting, and for the first time in months, I feel a hint of the famous Georgian warmth in the breeze.

We have the place mostly to ourselves. I suddenly get the feeling that she's going to take my hand, or maybe that I'm going to take hers, so I stuff my hands in my pockets.

"I suppose I should thank you, but I'm not sure how I feel about you hiding so much from me."

"I had to. Plausible deniability." It always sounded like such an excuse when Julep said it, but now I get it.

"Don't ever do it again."

"Okay." Easy enough to promise, since I can't imagine we'll be interacting much after this. I'm not exactly in her sphere. Besides, the job is over, and I have no intention of masterminding something like this ever again, much less forming a crew to do it regularly. I know now that I can do it, but it's not who I am. I'm a hacker. It's what I love the way Olson loves math.

"Are you ever going to tell me what happened to you in Chicago? About Julep?"

Holy topic change, Batman. Where is this coming from?

"There's not much else to—"

She waves me to silence. "Not about hacking for her or whatever. About how she broke your heart."

I don't know what to say to that. It's not a story for public consumption.

"I'm into math, you know, so it wasn't hard to put two and two together," she says, smiling sadly. "The way you talk about her—there was no way you were leaving her unless she broke your heart."

"It's not broken." Now that I'm adjusting to the topic, I find I don't mind telling her so much. I guess she's inspiring on more than one front. "It's just bruised a little."

"I'm glad to hear it. I was afraid you might object if I did this."

"Did wh—?"

Before I can finish the thought, she grabs my face, pulls me down an inch or so to meet her, and kisses me. On the lips. I'm so surprised that I don't know if I'm supposed to push her away or pull her closer. But she relaxes into me, her arms snaking around my neck, and my brain just shuts off altogether. My arms pull her body flush with mine and my mouth absorbs her taste. As the kiss deepens, I get flashes of thought—*good, wrong, want,* and *not Julep.*

She breaks the kiss, loosening her grip on me and letting out a shaky exhale.

"Damn," she whispers, resting her forehead against my chin. "That's pretty much as awesome as I thought it would be."

I have no idea what's happening right now. I have so many conflicting urges that I have no freaking clue what to do or say next. But I don't let her go. I don't push her away. I do kiss her softly on the forehead. It seems like the right thing to do.

"What are you thinking?" she asks.

I laugh, a little shaky myself. "I can't even tell you."

"Mm. That sounds naughty."

Does it? I replay the sentence in my mind. Crap, it does. I didn't mean it to.

"Katherine—"

She shivers in my arms. "It's official. You're never allowed to call me Olson again."

I close my eyes. She isn't making this easier. Maybe it would help if I let go of her. But I can't seem to convince my arms to do it.

"Katherine, you don't want to do this. I'm not a good option for you. I'm—"

"You're what?"

"I'm still bruised. And scarred, too. It's not just my heart. It's every part of me. I came here to escape, but I can't escape my past."

"No, but you can heal from it. And you can have help. You're allowed to be damaged. We all are."

I shake my head. "Not like this."

She presses her finger into my lips. "Are you trying to talk me out of liking you for my protection or for yours?"

"Both," I mumble past her finger. I move my head so I can speak more freely. "I don't want my hurt to hurt you."

"It already hurts me, Sam." She strokes my cheek, her blue eyes staring up with deep empathy into mine. "I already care about you. And there's nothing you or I can do about that now."

She kisses me again, and the hell with it, I let her.

But then my phone vibrates in my pocket.

She chuckles. "Wow. I knew I was good, but jeez."

"Ha-ha." I don't recognize the number, so I tap Ignore.

"Where were we?" she says.

"We were talking." I attempt to sound stern, but she's too high on the elation from earlier to listen to me.

She kisses me again, and the phone vibrates again.

"Seriously, who is calling you?"

"I don't know." I take the phone out again and frown at it. It's the same number. And what's weird is that I have my phone set to send unknown numbers straight to voicemail. It shouldn't be ringing through in the first place.

"Maybe you should answer it."

I silence it again and put it back in my pocket. "This is more important."

"It is, isn't it?" She smiles impishly and pulls me closer, but this time I push back.

"Wait."

But before I can get out what I'm trying to say, the phone vibrates again. She frowns. "I think you should take it. It seems important."

"All right. But I won't be long. We have to finish this."

"I like the sound of that."

I have no idea who the caller could be, but whoever's on the other end is getting my aggravated tone. I'm not in the mood for this.

"Sam?"

The woman's voice sounds vaguely familiar, but I can't place it.

"Yes?"

"This is Alessandra Dupree."

I fumble the phone, nearly dropping it. Julep's *mom*? Why the hell would Julep's mom be calling me?

"I'm sorry, could you say that again?"

"I know this is awkward, me calling out of the blue. But I need your help. My daughter needs your help."

Dozens of questions spring to mind. Why you? Why me? Why now? Why not call Mike, Julep's FBI handler and foster father? Or even Julep herself? And how could I possible help when I'm hundreds of miles away? And do I even want to? I still haven't accomplished what I came here to do.

But the idea of not knowing, of not helping is unthinkable. Which actually answers the question 'why me?' If Julep's mother is watching her enough to know she's in trouble, then she also knows how I feel about her, what I'd do for her. She knows that I'd move hell itself if it stood in my way.

Katherine watches me with concern, obviously picking up on my distress. But I can't worry about that now.

"What do you need me to do?" I say.

The End

WELLLL... not totally. Julep is back with her next installment *Trust Me, I'm Trouble* geni.us/trust meimtrouble. And this time, instead of the mob, she's going up against her own kind—another con artist. Will she be able to out-grift another grifter? Or will she lose her only connection to her long-lost mother?

To be notified when future Trust Me books are released, sign up for email updates at geni.us/theunder ground.

And if you enjoyed the story, please leave a review!

ABOUT THE AUTHOR

MARY ELIZABETH SUMMER (she/her) likes to poke at dark places until the light spills out, which is why her characters are constantly glaring at her and applying adhesive bandages. She is currently contributing to the delinquency of minors by writing books about a teen con artist solving mysteries by doing crime. She lives in Portland, Oregon with her daughter and small menagerie of pets. For email updates on new releases, sign up on maryelizabethsummer.com.

amazon.com/author/maryelizabethsummer

instagram.com/mesummerbooks

bsky.app/profile/mesummerbooks.bsky.social

bookbub.com/authors/mary-elizabeth-summer

ALSO BY MARY ELIZABETH SUMMER

Trust Me, I'm Lying (Trust Me series #1)

Down to the Liar (novella, Trust Me series #2)

Trust Me, I'm Trouble (Trust Me series #3)

Out of Sight (novella, Trust Me series #4)

Trust Me, I'm Trying (Trust Me series #5)

(Trust Me series #6, forthcoming)

(Trust Me series #7, forthcoming)

www.ingramcontent.com/pod-product-compliance
Lightning Source LLC
Chambersburg PA
CBHW031517010826
48973CB00013B/2638